Gail felt it was important that she make Jim understand.

She heard her own voice saying, "But I'd like you to know why. . .why I was upset. Why I've been so silly . . .working so hard."

The blue eyes went very dark. He turned his gaze back to the swimmers. "You don't have to if it upsets you too much. But sometimes it does help to talk it out." He hesitated, and then continued slowly. "Mum told me your brother was killed in a car accident. You limp sometimes at the end of a long day. Although I think not as much as when you first arrived." He paused again. "Were you driving the car?"

The soft query shook her. How dreadful if she had been! She swallowed hard.

"No," she said softly at last, "my father was driving."

He stiffened, but was silent. She took a deep breath and closed her eyes.

"I was the only survivor."

MARY HAWKINS lives with her husband in Australia; they have three grown children. Her mother and father were pioneer grain farmers on the Darling Downs in Queensland, Australia, the setting for *Search for Tomorrow*, her first inspirational novel.

Search
for Tomorrow

Mary Hawkins

Heartsong Presents

To Raymond. . .my chief encourager, best
friend, perfect lover, wonderful husband—
God's perfect gift.

ISBN 1-55748-426-0

SEARCH FOR TOMORROW

one

"They're here, Gail!" Ann said.

Abigail Brandon raised her bowed head and looked at her friend as she burst into the bedroom.

Ann took one look at Gail's face and her own cheerful, freckled features crinkled with laughter. "Gail! You've got to be kidding! You've been crying!"

Gail sniffed and wiped her eyes again. She glared at Ann. "Sympathetic friend you are," she began. The smile vanished from Ann Green's face and an anxious look appeared.

Gail relented. She jumped up from the bed and flung an arm around Ann's shoulders. "Oh, don't mind me. There's nothing really wrong. It's just. . ."

Ann hugged her. "I know," she said briefly, "I felt like that yesterday at the graduation service." Her eyes began to twinkle again. "Only I didn't get around to shedding any tears over it."

Gail moved over to the bare dressing table and peered into the mirror. She brushed the honey-colored curls off her forehead and reached for her bag. "Well," she said defensively as she began to repair her makeup, "I was all right until I walked back into this room after breakfast. All my luggage was gone and it just looked so. . . .so bare somehow." She turned and surveyed the small, sparsely furnished room. "I guess it all just hit me. Three years of

5

my life, in rooms like this one, are suddenly gone."

"And then you realized that it was wonderful!" Ann laughed again. "I should be the one shedding tears because I don't have an impatient fiancé waiting downstairs to take me away and marry me and set up our own happy home. Come on, or he'll be storming up here to find you."

"Ann, I know it's stupid, but. . . .," Gail swallowed on the lump rising in her throat again, "last night I was so thrilled and excited and now I'm really sorry the three years are over. I'm getting married next week and even when I come back here after our honeymoon as a fully fledged nursing sister, it's all going to be so different. You'll be gone, too, and so many of our friends, and—"

"And you'll be so happy with Wayne in your own home that you won't give us a second thought," Ann interrupted her abruptly. "If you don't stop being so soppy you'll have me in tears in a moment. Now, do get a move on."

She straightened the crumpled bedspread and waited impatiently near the door. Gail threw her makeup back in her bag and couldn't resist one last look around the room before following Ann out into the corridor.

The senior Clinical Nurse Educator was talking to Wayne James near the front entrance of the Nurses' Home that had been converted into low cost accommodations for students and other staff members of the hospital. They turned and smiled as the two women hurried toward them.

"Well, Sister Brandon, you're ready at last." Sister Jean Drew chuckled at the startled look on Gail's face. "Oh, I know you are now Miss Brandon, State Registered Nurse, but I'm afraid you'll still be called 'Sister' by us older generation of nurses. And if I don't call you that now I'll never get another chance. It'll be Sister James the next time I see you. I do wish you God's richest blessings for your wedding, my dear."

Gail caught the sudden gleam in Wayne's eyes, and color flooded her cheeks. Somehow, she found herself murmuring the correct responses and farewells. Then, Wayne was holding her hand and hurrying her outside towards her father's green Holden Commodore sedan.

"Boy, Abbey! We've been waiting for ages. I thought you'd be waiting on the doorstep for us." Her brother Bill's excited face appeared at the back window. From the front seat, Mrs. Brandon smiled understandingly at her daughter as Wayne opened the back door.

He hesitated, and said to Gail's father, "Sure you wouldn't like me to drive, Mr. Brandon?"

"No, no. Not until we're over the mountains, Wayne. You can drive the last hundred or so kilometers." He grinned at Gail. "You sit in the back and keep that daughter of mine in order for a while."

Gail smiled back at him. Love for her family flooded through her. They had always been close, and Gail had hated leaving them and the large country town to do her nurse's training in Sydney. When Wayne appeared on the scene, she saw even less of them. But, they had welcomed him as her choice and lovingly helped her in every way to plan for their wedding that was now only two weeks away. She started to climb into the back seat when she thought of something. "Are you sure you packed that small red case in the boot, Dad?"

"Of course he has, silly," Wayne said from behind her. He caught at her arm and pulled her from the car. "Come

on, I'll get in first and sit in the center. You can wave
goodbye to the old place from the window. And, seeing
that you get travel sick so often on those bends over the
Blue Mountains. . . ."

As the car moved off, they all waved to Ann. They
continued to gently tease Gail as they traveled to join the
stream of traffic on the Western Freeway.

The conversation gradually turned toward the graduation ceremony at the university and the special dinner that
was held after it. Gail answered their comments and
questions about the various people they had met and seen.
Over the years, they had heard Gail speak of some of them,
but they had found it very interesting to see them "in the
flesh" as Bill put it.

"Old Sister Drew doesn't seem too bad," said Gail's
mother. "I remember how scared you were of her three
years ago during your first clinical experience in the wards
and you expected to meet a real old dragon."

"Well, she's changed these last couple of years. They
say she never misses going to church now. We think God
must have tamed her."

Gail's flippant words created a little pool of silence
instead of the expected, automatic rebuke that such a
mention of God would have brought from Gail's mother
or father.

"We haven't missed church for a while ourselves," Mrs.
Brandon said so quietly that for a moment Gail thought she
must have misunderstood her. She turned and cocked an
eyebrow at Wayne, but he was looking at her a little
anxiously.

Before she could speak, Bill leaned forward across

Wayne and touched his mother's shoulder. "Don't you think we could tell Abbey now, Mum?"

Mrs. Brandon turned and exchanged a glance with Wayne.

"What on earth do you need to tell me now that you couldn't have told me last night?" Gail's laugh was a little uneasy. There was something in the atmosphere in the car that she couldn't quite put her finger on. "Have you some deep, dark secret, Bill?"

"No, it's not really a secret, darling." Mrs. Brandon looked reproachfully at her son. "Bill, you know we agreed to let Wayne tell her in his own good time."

"That's right, you young terror." Wayne's clasp on Gail's hand tightened and his smile seemed a little forced.

Suddenly, Gail knew that whatever he was going to tell her would be important. "Good grief! You all sound so mysterious," said Gail.

"Don't look so alarmed, Abbey." Wayne pretended to duck as he used the forbidden nickname only Bill was still allowed to use, mainly because Gail had given up trying to stop him. Although Gail tilted her chin at him in the way they played this game, she had the strangest feeling he was thinking hard about something else, and she felt a hint of alarm that did not entirely disappear as Wayne slipped his arm around her for a quick hug.

"It's really something very wonderful that's happened," Wayne said. "I'll tell you when we get home. Now, what's so special about that small red case?"

Gail frowned at the decisive tone in his voice as he changed the subject. But the wedding dress in that small red case had been picked up from the dressmaker only a couple of days before, and her eyes lit up at the thought of it.

They were still discussing clothes and plans for the wedding some time later after the freeway was behind them and the Holden was swinging around the sharp curves in the mountain roads. Bill had gradually dropped out of the general conversation and was sitting forward, behind his father, watching the road and trying to anticipate when Mr. Brandon would have to change gears as the car climbed steadily upward. He was becoming more and more fascinated with the thought of learning to drive and was already allowed to drive the small tractor around the orchard.

Gail noticed his rapt attention and touched her mother, nodding silently towards Bill. Mrs. Brandon winked at her, and they grinned at each other.

"Gail, there are some goodies to chew in that bag on the floor near your feet," Mrs. Brandon said. "I'm sure a certain young man with hollow legs must be feeling a little hungry by now."

Gail felt around the floor near their feet, but the bag had somehow been kicked under the front seat. She unfastened her seat belt and leaned down. She heard Wayne start to protest when a startled cry came from Bill.

"Wow, Dad! That semi! It's coming—"

Gail heard his voice rise to a scream that suddenly mingled with and was lost in the tortured screech of brakes. She felt her body being thrown down onto the floor into a tangled heap. Almost simultaneously, the world exploded into screeching, grinding metal and violent movement. Searing pain reached out to clutch her and the noise, at last, faded into darkness.

Once, she felt rough hands pulling at her body. Someone was shouting again, over and over. A sudden roar cut off the frantic voice. A wave of heat hit her. Pain was swamping her, but the relentless hands wouldn't let her go. Someone was screaming again and then the pain engulfed her until she slid thankfully back into the welcome blackness.

two

Gail walked quickly up the steps and into the old red brick building. Its neat sign still told the world it was the ROYAL HOSPITAL NURSES' HOME although it had been several years since the switch from hospital to college training that meant that not only nurses now occupied the building. She was neatly dressed in matching amber slacks and jacket. A close observer would have noticed the slight favoring of her left leg as she swung down the corridor leading to Sister Jean Drew's office. It was the only outward sign of the weeks spent in the hospital and the long convalescence since the accident. Her mind was in a turmoil.

A few days ago, she had been so relieved to be told she could start work again that she had eagerly rung the hospital and made an appointment to see the Director of Nursing. Now, her cheeks were still flushed after that interview with Miss Fisher. Tears were not far from her brown eyes as she hesitated outside the Nurse Educator's office.

What on earth am I going to do now? she thought.

She fought down a rising tide of panic and lifted her hand to knock on the door, but it suddenly swung back and Sister Jean Drew briskly welcomed her.

"Oh, there you are, Sister Brandon. I was just beginning to wonder if Miss Fisher remembered to give you my message. Do come in for a few minutes. I haven't seen you since your discharge from the hospital."

Before she could voice a protest, Gail found herself ushered in and seated in the room's only comfortable chair. The last thing she felt like doing was to have a session with Sister Drew! But, when she saw the morning tea tray neatly arranged on the desk, she realized there was no escape. She had come only because Sister had been so kind to her all through those lonely, black days. She quickly tossed off that thought, as she had forced herself to do so many times since leaving the safety of the hospital ward. She couldn't dare let herself dwell on those nightmarish days.

Sister Jean Drew had been busy pouring boiling water into the teapot and, as she returned to her desk, she said, "Although it's nearly lunch time, I knew you'd feel like a cup of tea after seeing Miss Fisher."

So she knew, Gail thought grimly and waited silently.

Sister Drew was noted for not beating about the bush and, as she efficiently dealt with cups and saucers, she came straight to the point. "I understand that Miss Fisher finds herself unable to employ you for some months."

"Did she tell you why, Sister?" Gail couldn't keep the resentment from creeping into her low, attractive voice.

Sister Jean Drew glanced at her sharply. Then she frowned, as though Gail had confirmed a thought of hers. "Er, well, yes. She told me that she'd had to fill the original position she had intended to keep for you after graduation." As she poured their tea, she continued in a gentler voice. "Also, I believe your last doctor's report did not wholeheartedly recommend that you were fit enough for ward work yet."

"Well, Doctor Wentworth told me I could start work, but apparently told Miss Fisher that all bones were mended but not. . .not my mind, and my. . .my memory. . . ."

The attempt at flippancy failed miserably. Gail bit her lip, and stared down at her tightly clenched hands. No! She mustn't cry here!

"Both your body and mind have certainly taken a whipping these past few months," Sister Drew said crisply. "I know Miss Fisher did not decide hastily or lightly that you needed more time to adjust."

Adjust had not been the word the Director of Nursing had used, thought Gail grimly. Her fingernails were biting into the palms of her hands as the quiet, reluctant tones of Miss Fisher's voice echoed again in her ears.

"In one dreadful experience, you have lost the people you most loved—your parents, brother, fiancé." Miss Fisher had swallowed quickly, and then looked away for a moment. "Too dreadful to think about!" she had murmured before continuing firmly, "Apparently you are still having a few nightmares. How can you be expected to be emotionally and mentally stable enough to be put in charge of a ward full of very sick, dependent people?"

Gail suddenly realized Sister Drew was waiting for her to take the proffered cup of steaming tea. Numbly, she unclasped her hands and reached out to take it. She made a conscious effort to control the trembling hand that shook so much that some of the tea spilled into the saucer.

"Milk and sugar, Sister Brandon?"

The voice was crisp and businesslike. When Gail shook her head silently, not at that moment trusting her voice, Sister Drew just politely handed her a plate of cake. "Sister

Brandon, have you ever given any thought to the wisdom of getting right away from Sydney for a while?"

Gail felt as though food would choke her. She managed to politely refuse the cake and sipped a mouthful of the hot drink, hoping it might help to dislodge the hard lump in her throat. At last, she raised her head and managed to look directly at the woman standing near her. "Run away, you mean, Sister?"

Sister Drew frowned slightly at the hint of bitterness in Gail's voice. "You need to get away and start a new life. Here, you have too many painful memories." She paused. Gail felt she may as well have said, "and your mind can't cope with them yet." Instead, Sister Drew continued, "I don't think you can call that running away, just common sense."

"But where could I go? Jobs are so hard to get now, and I need to work. I must work." Gail saw concern flash into the older woman's faded blue eyes and added quickly, "Oh, I don't mean I'm short of money. In fact, when . . .when Dad's estate's finalized, I'll have more than enough. It's just that I've had nothing to do but think these last few ghastly months. I thought it would be easier when I came back. But now. . .I don't know what to do. I must find something to do. Somewhere to live!"

An edge of panic had crept into Gail's voice, and it did not escape the experienced ears of the older woman. "I believe you spent your convalescence with your mother's sister. Is there no chance of staying on there for a while?"

"No." Gail's answer was abrupt, final.

Sister Drew looked at her thoughtfully, hesitated for a moment, and then moved around her desk and sat down.

Her back was very straight as she stared at Gail.

Gail suspected that Aunt Harriet must have rung Miss Fisher about the nightmares Gail had experienced during the week. As she wondered how she could explain Aunt Harriet to Sister Drew, Gail was tense and still. She knew that the hospital staff had been relieved when they had been told that Gail was going straight to her aunt's when she was discharged.

Aunt Harriet had been an unknown quantity to Gail. During the past few years, Mrs. Brandon had seen very little of her only sister. After Gail had been living in the cold, perfectly kept house for a few days, she knew why.

She was a childless widow to whom the impression that others had of her was the vital factor in her life. Very active in her local church, she was a woman "full of good works," but with a heart that Gail had discovered lacked any real warmth and affection. Gail had soon begun to realize that one of her aunt's main aims in life was to make sure people knew how religious she was by her ceaseless involvement in the activities of her local church and district social service organizations.

Gail shuddered as she remembered the final confrontation with her aunt last night. Since it was Gail's last night, Aunt Harriet had apparently decided it was her duty to "have a little chat" with her poor bereft niece before seeing her back off into the hard, cruel world. Many pious platitudes had flowed forth and Gail had at first endured them with a suitable demeanor.

The final straw had come when Aunt Harriet had put her carefully manicured, heavily ringed hand on Gail's arm and said, "And of course, my dear, you must try harder to accept what has happened. If you would only get involved in the church, I'm sure it would help. God is love, and—"

Gail had rounded on her. "Accept what has happened! I don't want to have anything to do with your God or your church!" She had almost choked with fury. "You're nothing but an old humbug, and a hypocrite as well! I haven't seen one thing here, or elsewhere, to make me want to get involved in religion. And I won't listen to another word, Aunt Harriet!"

Sister Drew had been silently studying the girl who was lost in thought. Her weeks of convalescence had done little to restore color to the thin, drawn face. Gail heard a sigh and looked up. She shrugged as she saw the look directed at her.

"No," Gail said again. When Sister Drew raised an eyebrow inquiringly, she blurted out, "She's too religious for me," and then bit her lip in embarrassment as the suggestion of a twinkle appeared briefly in the kind eyes watching her intently. She remembered the gossip about the reason Sister Drew had changed from the cranky, fault finding disciplinarian they had all been scared of to this warm woman, who was always so concerned about her "girls."

Gail felt relieved when her remark was ignored as Sister Drew leaned forward in her chair and picked up a couple of sheets of paper from her desk. "Well, if that's the case, I may be able to help you and an old friend at the same time."

Gail turned and looked intently at Sister Drew, who was fiddling with the papers in her hand.

"I received this letter a couple of days ago from the son of a very old and dear friend of mine, Marian Stevens, who suffers from periodic attacks of asthma," Sister Drew continued. "I knew she had been in and out of the hospital several times this year. Now Jim, her son, tells me she's just recovering from an attack of pneumonia as well. The family's had one misfortune after another. Some years ago, her husband and eldest son jointly bought the property where they now live. They had to take out a mortgage to help pay for it, and were still battling to pay it off when John, Marian's husband, was killed. Since then, things have been rather difficult for them financially."

Sister Drew paused. When she hesitantly continued, Gail felt she was choosing her words very carefully.

"Earlier this year, she wrote and told me her daughter's husband had walked out after a bitter quarrel and they didn't know where he was. Then, some. . .er. . .time ago, she wrote and said they had been informed that he had been seriously injured."

Gail was beginning to feel a little puzzled. Sister Drew had not once looked directly at her, was still fidgeting about, and altogether was not at all like her usual direct self. For some reason Gail began to be more and more uneasy. She forced herself to remain silent as Sister Drew quickly continued.

"The daughter immediately left her two children with Marian and Jim and rushed off to be with her husband, hoping for a reconciliation. The husband's. . .er. . .injury is apparently going to mean a long period in the hospital.

My friend ended up in the hospital herself with this pneumonia and, since then, Jim's had the sole responsibility of the children and, of course, his younger brother, Will. From what I can gather, neighbors have rallied around and he has coped reasonably well. But, now it seems that Marian is fretting to come home. It'll be harvest time in a few weeks, and Jim's afraid she'll try to do too much and trigger off more asthma attacks. He's asked me if I know of a reliable woman I could recommend who'd be able to go and help them out at such short notice. He's warned me they can't afford a very large salary and he hasn't a clue how long he'll need help. He has to get someone as soon as possible, as Marian's doctor has agreed to let her out this weekend if suitable arrangements can be made." The words had gradually quickened to a virtual torrent. Sister Drew took a deep breath, and almost flung the next words at Gail. "Do you think you could possibly consider taking the position?"

Gail stared at her with increasing apprehension. "But . . .but. . .Sister Drew, I'm a trained nurse, not a housekeeper. I can't even cook! Surely, your friend doesn't need any nursing care."

Sister Drew relaxed slightly. "Well, Jim didn't say anything about that in his letter," she admitted reluctantly. "But I would certainly feel happier knowing there was someone in the house with some professional knowledge. Marian's also a victim of arthritis. But don't you think a complete change of lifestyle may help you, too?"

Gail studied her thoughtfully. "It mightn't be such a change as you think. We. . .we lived on a farm. Where do your friends live?"

"Oh, how silly of me! I should have told you that first of all. I'm afraid it's in Queensland."

"Queensland!"

"Yes. I believe it's about a thousand kilometers north of us, well over a hundred kilometers west of Brisbane. Have you ever heard of the Darling Downs?"

"Isn't Toowoomba on the Darling Downs?"

"Why, yes. It's called the 'Queen city of the Darling Downs' or 'The Garden City.' Their property's some distance west of there."

The Garden City. The Carnival of Flowers.

Gail stood up abruptly. Blindly, she moved across to the open window.

She could hear her mother's excited voice saying, "Harold, we must try and have a trip to Toowoomba. They say it's the most beautiful city. The whole place gets ready for a Carnival of Flowers every September. Apparently it's unbelievably beautiful. Do let's try and go!"

The trip had been planned for this year. Now, it was November. And her parents would never go anywhere. . . .

Sister Drew sat rigidly in her chair. There had been sheer agony in Gail's dark brown eyes. She had desperately wanted to go to her and had even started to stand, before sinking back helplessly onto her chair as Gail had moved away. She closed her eyes tightly, and her lips moved soundlessly in a desperate prayer. "Dear God. Please. Please help her. Only let her agree if You know it's the best way for her and the Stevenses!"

So much depended on the next few moments. For hours last night, Sister Drew had lain awake praying and planning. She looked down at her clenched fist. Deliberately, she relaxed her grip and straightened out the crumpled pages of the letter. She pushed back her chair and slowly stood up.

The noise penetrated Gail's memories. She turned and looked at Sister Drew. Gails's eyes were burning and dry, but she had control of herself again.

Compassion made Sister Drew's voice very gentle. "My dear, I know you'd like time to think this over but, unfortunately, I need to know straight away. Jim followed this letter with a phone call last night. He's flying to Sydney today, but has to return tomorrow. If you decide you don't want to go, I will have to make other arrangements."

Gail put her fingers to each side of her pale cheeks. "I don't know that I have much choice."

At the desolation and pain in Gail's voice, Sister Drew walked quickly over to her.

"Do you think I could meet him first?" asked Gail. "He might not think I'd be suitable."

As she finished speaking, Gail felt Sister Drew's hand rest gently on her stooped shoulders and saw understanding and caring in her eyes.

"I'm afraid he sounded so desperate, anyone I can persuade to go would be 'suitable.' I'm not sure about meeting him. He's here on urgent family business and will be dreadfully rushed for time."

Gail interrupted her. "Have you said anything to him about me?"

"Why, no. As a matter of fact, he rang me just before Miss Fisher saw me last night and told me about you."

Sister Drew smiled a little ruefully at the expression on Gail's face. "Yes, I'm afraid I did know all about it. Miss Fisher is very concerned about you."

Gail moved away and shrugged her shoulders slightly. "You're both probably right. It was just so. . .so disappointing. But what I'm wondering is, does he have to know about the accident?" A strange expression flashed across Sister Drew's face. For a moment, Gail wondered if she had imagined it. She hurried on, "You see, I find it so. . .so awful. It either embarrasses people, and they don't know what to say, or else they," she gulped, "they say too much. I would feel more at ease if they treated me just like anyone else."

Sister Drew was staring thoughtfully at Gail. "I wonder," she began very slowly. "Gail, do you think you would take it one step farther and even change your name slightly? You see," she hurriedly added as Gail's eyes widened, "they may have read, or heard about the accident and remembered your name. When you get to know them, I'm sure you'll want to tell them. But. . .but. . .at your own leisure," she finished rather weakly.

Gail stared. That the day would ever have come when upright, straight-from-the-shoulder Sister Drew would suggest such a thing!

A touch of color tinged Sister Drew's cheeks as she read the amazement in Gail's face. She avoided looking at Gail as she added, "He doesn't even need to know you're a trained nurse if you like. He may wonder why on earth a trained nurse wants to take on a job like this." Sister Drew stopped abruptly.

Gail began to feel more uneasy about the whole thing. "I don't know," she said hesitantly, "there could be all kinds of complications. My lawyers haven't finished sorting out all. . .all the business yet, and—"

"Oh, I could forward all your mail to you," Sister Drew said eagerly.

There was silence. They looked at each other. Gail's brown eyes were very dark. The older, pale blue eyes looking into hers were pleading. They even seemed to be asking for more than her words had expressed. Gail shook off the fanciful thought. She straightened. A reckless expression lightened her face. Her chin tilted. After all, what did it matter? What did anything matter any more?

"Okay, Sister Drew. From now on I'm Gail Brand, not Abigail Brandon as the news reports called me. Surely, after nearly four months, that will be enough."

Relieved, Sister Drew closed her eyes for a moment. "Oh, my dear! Yes, that should do it. They really are a delightful family and I'm sure it won't be long before you'll feel free to tell them your real name." Suddenly, she became her usual businesslike self and moved briskly back to the desk. "Look, let's sit down again and sort out some of the details. How soon do you think you could go?"

"As soon as it takes me to get my luggage from the cloakroom at Central Station," Gail said a little grimly. At Sister Drew's raised eyebrows, she added, "You see, the train was late, so I just left them there and caught a taxi straight here. I thought that once I was sure of being allocated a room here I could go back and pick them up then. Now, I can take them to a motel room. I couldn't very well leave them at the entrance to the Nursing Administration offices."

Sister Drew's lips twitched. "Not very well," she murmured. "I don't think there's a vacancy here at the moment. When I see Jim I'll ask him, but I wouldn't be surprised if he jumps at the chance to take you with him tomorrow. It would save an extra trip from their farm to Brisbane to pick you up." She paused, and said hesitantly, "There. . .there's no one you have to visit before you leave?"

"No. Ann—Sister Green—has gone, and I don't feel like coping with anyone else at the moment."

Sister Drew hesitated again. She picked up a pen and started to doodle with it before looking up intently at Gail. Gail stiffened. She suddenly suspected what Sister Drew was thinking.

"Gail, I wondered if you'd given any more thought about visiting that unfortunate young man I spoke to you about before you were discharged?"

Gail's lips tightened and remained stubbornly closed. She looked away.

"He's still paralyzed, my dear," Sister Drew said sadly. "Isn't that enough punishment?"

She waited silently and, when Gail eventually spoke, her voice was very low, but the bitterness and anger made Sister Drew wince.

"So he's paralyzed. Unfortunate man? He was drunk! Because of that, he wiped out a car full of people—my people! He had no right to be driving that truck. I'm not going to see him. I think I would probably try to kill him if I did." She stared defiantly at Sister Drew.

The color drained from the wrinkled cheeks of Sister

Drew, who suddenly looked stricken as she jumped to her feet. Gail thought she muttered something like "what have I done?" as her pen clattered down on the desk.

"I know you vowed something similar before. But I hoped. . .I. . .you. . .I hoped you might be feeling a little differently now that the. . .the shock has had time to. . .to . . ." Sister Drew gulped and came to an abrupt halt. Then she added, almost to herself, "But I hadn't dreamed how deep the bitterness had gone."

Gail had refused to let anyone even mention Arthur Smith's name during those first black days after she had been told why the ones she longed for the most never visited her. Only Sister Drew, in her usual forthright way, had at last dared to insist on telling Gail about him.

There had been a severe injury to his spinal cord. Extensive tests had eventually shown that it was not completely severed, but he remained paralyzed from the waist down. He still had not shown any improvement after a couple of apparently successful operations.

Sister Drew had even told her how he had begged and pleaded with the doctors to let him die when he had first realized that he had been responsible for the death of four people. Later, he had pleaded to be taken to see Gail, but she had always refused. It had become an obsession with him and he begged and pleaded so much that, just before Gail's discharge, Sister Drew had confronted her again, telling her there was something he insisted she should know, something he would not tell anyone else.

Gail had looked her old Nursing Educator in the eye with a cold, uncompromising "No," and then turned away without another word.

"Oh, my poor dear. Please don't harbor such bitterness," Sister Drew now implored her. "An unforgiving spirit can twist and warp your soul, and—"

A loud rap on the door prevented Gail from blurting out hot, angry words. Sister Drew bit her lip and frowned. She moved toward the door, hesitated, and then turned as though to say something more. She looked at the compressed lips, the flushed cheeks, and furious eyes. With a sigh of defeat, Sister Drew opened the door.

A tall, dark-haired man in a dark brown suit stood in the doorway. His face lit up in a warm, affectionate grin. Two large hands reached out to give Sister Drew a huge hug that was followed by a light kiss.

"Hello, Aunt Jean."

"Jim!"

It hardly needed Sister Drew's muffled exclamation to warn Gail that this was her new employer.

"I'm sorry if I'm interrupting you," the deep tones began and then cut off as he looked over his Aunt's head and saw Gail. His eyes lit with a glint of appreciation for a beautiful woman. Then, his smile stilled for a moment as he studied with interest the flushed cheeks and the anger that still lingered in her attractive features.

His glance was suddenly piercing and it brought Gail to her feet. She felt added warmth leap to her face as he continued to stare at her while Sister Drew ushered him in and closed the door.

"I thought I'd just let you know I've arrived." He turned his attention back to his Aunt. "Beth's outside in a hired car, so I can't stay."

"Oh, Jim, it is good to see you. I've been so concerned

for you all." Sister Drew broke off and gestured toward Gail, who was more than a little flustered. "Before you race off, I want you to meet a young friend of mine. Gail. . . ," she paused for a second as though a little undecided, and then said distinctly, "Gail Brand. This is the Jim Stevens we've just been talking about, Gail."

Gail extended her hand to meet the large one stretched out to her. It tingled as it was taken firmly by the strong, deeply tanned hand of the man still staring at her. She felt a little dazed and hardly realized her new name had been used for the first time.

He must be well over six feet! she thought. *He should have dark brown eyes to match his brown face, brown hair, and brown suit,* she thought ridiculously. Instead, clear, bright blue eyes twinkled down at her. Then, the twinkle faded and the eyes darkened. They seemed to be searching out her very soul. He wasn't merely seeing her well-shaped features and the short, honey brown curls that now bounced around her face in gay abandon. She knew by his suddenly serious expression that he had recognized the strain in her darkly ringed eyes and the tightly controlled smile that had briefly tilted her shapely mouth.

After a moment, he allowed the twinkle back, and smiled gently at her. "Talking about me, was she, Gail? Well, don't believe everything she says, will you?"

"Jim!" Sister Drew's exclamation was so sharp they both turned quickly toward her. Red crept into Sister Drew's cheeks as they stared at her in surprise. Her eyes were filled with distress. The fingers of one hand were pressed to her lips.

Gail's uneasiness returned with a rush. Sister Drew was behaving completely out of character.

Jim whistled softly. "Wow! If ever anyone looked an absolute picture of guilt! What on earth have you been saying, Aunt Jean?"

"Well, I...er...we..." Sister Drew broke off, and Jim's teasing smile disappeared. He gave her his sudden piercing look. She took a deep breath and, with a touch of defiance said, "Why, about your problem with the children and your mother, of course. I've just managed to persuade Gail to go and help you out."

Jim looked taken aback and a little dismayed. He recovered swiftly and, with an embarrassed laugh, he said, "Well, that's great. But Aunt Jean, I was hoping...that is, well, you...Mum very much wants you to come."

Gail opened her mouth, but Sister Drew said rapidly, "No, I'm afraid that's out of the question this time. In fact," she continued crisply, "Gail has just told me that as her previous plans have unexpectedly fallen through, she is quite able and willing to return with you."

Jim looked doubtfully at Gail. "Did she tell you what little terrors the children can be, and that—"

"Don't worry," Sister Drew interrupted him. "Gail is very capable and can cope. I wouldn't have asked her otherwise. Didn't you say Beth was outside, Jim?"

"Good grief, yes." The slight drawl that had been in his deep tones before disappeared. He straightened abruptly. "In fact, she's driving round and round because we couldn't get a parking space within a kilometer of here. I told her I'd only be a few minutes. So, unfortunately, there's no more time to talk this out. We're going flat hunting before the next visiting hours." His brisk voice paused, and then continued a shade apologetically, "Aunt Jean, I actually called in to see if you could come as soon as possible, and to apologize for not coming to tea tonight, because I want to catch this evening's plane back."

Sister Drew gave an exclamation of protest and dismay that he ignored. He turned to Gail and shot at her, "I guess that rules out any idea of your coming back with me."

To her own surprise, Gail felt something within her rise to meet the challenge in his keen eyes and brisk words.

"Not necessarily," she said coldly. She heard her voice match his for crispness. "My cases are still at Central Railway Station. It's just a matter of picking them up on the way to the airport."

A glint of something like admiration as well as curiosity touched the brilliant blue eyes intently studying her, but he didn't voice any of the obvious questions. He suddenly rubbed the palm of his hand over his face and then decisively picked up a pen from the desk and scribbled on a note pad.

"There. That's the flight number. Perhaps you could ring through and book Gail's seat for us, Aunt Jean. Must go. See you in the flight lounge, Gail." A quick hug for his aunt and he was gone.

As the door closed behind him, the two women looked at each other. Simultaneously, they smiled. Sister Drew suddenly realized it was the first real smile she had seen on Gail's face since that last day with Wayne.

"Phew! Is he always like that?"

"You mean, like a sudden squall blowing in and out? By no means. He must have a lot to do today with Beth." A shadow drove away the smile on Sister Drew's face and she abruptly continued as though she sensed the questions hovering on Gail's lips. "Well, I'm afraid I must get on, too. I'll ring the booking office and then I'd better do some of the work this hospital pays me to do."

Gail knew she was being gently dismissed, so she stood silently while the booking was being made. She longed to ask who Beth was. Jim had flown all that way apparently to help her.

I must be mad, she thought suddenly as Sister Drew put down the phone. *I can't possibly just fly off like this to people I know so very little about.*

Sister Drew seemed to sense her sudden panic and, without giving Gail a chance to speak, handed her the piece of paper with the flight number and departure time written on it as well as some money. Almost before she realized it, Gail found herself being ushered to the door. Sister Drew brought her brisk instructions to a close and unexpectedly kissed Gail on the cheek.

"Gail, dear, please write to me and let me know how you are getting on." Her voice revealed all her depth of compassion behind the professional front. She hesitated for a moment and, as Gail found herself too moved by the unexpected gesture to say a word, she heard Sister Drew say anxiously, "I know you'll find a true home and friends with the Stevenses. You might find it unexpectedly difficult to tell them who you are and, if so, do tell me and I'll help all I can. And, if by some chance it all doesn't work out, never forget that God loves you so very, very much, and there will be a home for you somewhere, someplace."

She smiled a little unsteadily at Gail and turned to reenter her office, leaving Gail even more apprehensive but with no option but to turn and walk away.

three

The rest of the afternoon, Gail was a turmoil of indecision and trepidation as she wandered around Sydney's inner city shops until it was time to collect her luggage and head for the airport. A couple of times she was on the verge of ringing Sister Drew to say she had changed her mind. But what alternative did she have?

Reluctantly, she at last hailed a taxi but her eyes remained tightly closed for the whole trip as she sat tensely in the back seat. She ignored the driver's smirk as she paid him. It was none of his business that travel in any car still made her stomach churn and her legs tremble. Let him think it was his prowess in negotiating Sydney's horrible peak hour traffic.

She lingered in the airport terminal's coffee shop as long as possible. When she went to the departure lounge, Jim Stevens was nowhere to be seen.

"A home for you. . .somewhere, someplace." Sister Drew's words flowed unbidden into her mind as a wave of weariness swept through her.

A home. She had no home. . .no family, no loved ones, no one who really cared. No, perhaps that wasn't quite right. For some reason Sister Drew had seemed to care what happened to her. She was still puzzled about that ridiculous name change idea. Surely, who she was couldn't matter to these strangers. A deep, desperate longing swept through her to find a home somewhere, a future. Home had always been where people who loved each other lived together, teased each other, sometimes argued fiercely, but always knew they were loved and accepted...and were together.

Loneliness, with all its horror and fear, began to grip her tired mind and she jumped up to peer out of the window overlooking the Tarmac. Reluctantly, she knew that Miss Fisher and Sister Drew were right about her mind not being healed. The nightmares and the fear of traveling in cars probably meant that some patient's injuries could impair her professional ability.

Gail deliberately switched her thoughts to her new employer. She tried to remember all that Sister Drew had said about him and his mother. Sister Drew had certainly been very keen for her to work for them. She stared with unseeing eyes out at the lights of the airport, remembering what Sister Drew had been trying to say when Jim had interrupted them.

Arthur Smith. She didn't want to think about him, nor those dreadful weeks in hospital, nor the accident.

As she had gradually surfaced from the fog of pain-killing drugs, the nursing staff had tried to keep any news of the accident from her. But it had been too late. They didn't know she had regained consciousness just long enough to have her brain seared by a repeat of one of the "on the spot" interviews. Another patient's radio had been left on and, at first, she had felt only mildly irritated at being disturbed until she had suddenly heard her own name mentioned.

And then, "They think the semi must have been drifting

all over the road. The poor people in that car didn't have a chance. The driver of the semi was drunk, of course."

Later, she had refused to accept any other accounts of the accident. The police had told her the truck's brakes had failed. She had looked at them with cold, angry eyes and said nothing. A drunk had wiped out her family and future, and she wished that the person who had dragged her from the crushed and burning car just in time had left her to die, too. The police hadn't been able to establish just how she had escaped from the tangled wreckage, but had been certain her injuries would have made it impossible for her do so without help.

"Miss Brand? Gail!"

A hand touched her shoulder and she turned dazed, agonized eyes to look straight into the penetrating blue of distant horizons.

"Afraid it's time to go," said Jim Stevens.

People were moving toward the exit. Jim Stevens put his hand under her elbow as she stumbled slightly. Their seat allocations were not together, and Jim smiled briefly at her as they separated.

Gail's limp was worse by the time Jim joined her again in Brisbane. With scarcely a word, he helped her collect her cases on a trolley before ushering her out of the brightly lit terminal. With a few muttered words of explanation, he left her with her things while he went for his car.

His car. He had left his car here all day. Tension mounted higher as she waited, watching others hurrying away into the darkness. An early model Holden Commodore slid into the curb. It was exactly the same color and model as. . .as. . . .

She gasped and began to tremble as Jim climbed out of the driver's seat and walked around to open the boot. She closed her eyes for a moment, but when she opened them the green car was still there.

She didn't notice the sharp, concerned glance that Jim gave her as he picked up one of the cases.

"You must be very tired," he said quietly. "Why don't you sit in the car and relax while I stow these things away."

"No!"

The word was barely more than a whisper as she turned from staring at the car to look at him. Jim's forehead creased for a moment. He hesitated.

"I'm all right." She tried to clear her throat, fighting for control.

Even to her own ears she sounded a little panic stricken and hoped that perhaps this handsome guy would think she was only getting cold feet at the thought of trusting herself to a stranger.

"Why don't you stretch out on the back seat then and have a sleep for a while."

Gail drew a ragged breath. She opened her mouth then closed it again and shook her head vigourously.

"No, no," she managed to gasp after failing miserably to control her trembling. "Definitely not the back."

Jim stared silently at her for a moment and then, without further comment, slammed the door closed again and opened the front one. It was as though her limbs were frozen to the spot. Then she felt his warm hand on her arm and, with a feeling of helplessness, let him guide her into the car.

She sat bolt upright and didn't move an inch as the car

pulled away from the curb.

"Afraid the trip will take nearly three hours," Jim said as they stopped at a set of traffic lights. He glanced at her, and when she still didn't move said very gently, "Look, I don't know what you're afraid of, but you'd better do your seat belt up before an irate policeman stops me."

A sudden thought jolted through Gail. Seat belt. There had been something about a seat belt. Wayne's voice. Why couldn't she remember those last precious moments before the smash?

Jerkily, she moved at last and, with stiff fingers, fumbled with the seat belt. She was vaguely aware that Jim was still watching her until the lights changed.

"We'll stop off somewhere and have a cup of coffee," he said in a soothing voice when she stiffened up again as the car moved forward. "When we get home I'll drop you off first before I go over to the neighbors to pick up the kids."

The words hardly registered. She sat as though frozen to the seat, scarcely aware of him or his growing concern. Jim concentrated on driving through a patch of heavy traffic for a while and, when she still hadn't moved, began to quietly point out places of interest. Not even the large bridge over the wide Brisbane River drew her gaze from the lights of the oncoming traffic.

Gail's stomach started heaving as the car's speed increased. She dreaded the open road. The only thing that made the nightmare bearable at all was that it was night time and she wouldn't be able see the semitrailers bearing down on them until they roared past.

Suddenly, Jim flicked on his indicators and pulled into

a brightly lit service station.

"I think this'll be a good spot for some petrol and that cup of coffee," Jim said as the car rolled to a stop.

Relief brought the taste of bile to Gail's mouth, and she wrenched open the door just in time.

Jim gave a sharp exclamation. A moment later Gail felt gentle hands helping her from the car, holding her head, as his distressed voice murmured, "You poor kid. Why didn't you say? You must have been feeling sick in the plane."

He waited until she had stopped heaving before he thrust a large handkerchief into her hand and then pulled her slight body to lean against his tall frame.

"Let's go and find a chair for you and something to settle your poor old stomach," he murmured softly when she at last stirred and moved back from him.

A sympathetic attendant managed to supply a glass of water and some antacid and, before long, Gail was feeling much better, although very much ashamed and embarrassed.

I guess Miss Fisher was definitely right after all, she thought grimly. *If I react like this to the car, what would happen if a severely burned patient were admitted to my ward?*

Jim's voice stopped that dreadful line of thought.

"Feeling better?" He was smiling sympathetically at her.

"I'm so sorry," she faltered, "you've been very kind."

His eyes twinkled at her over his coffee cup as he took a sip. "The children have given me rather a lot of practice these past few months with people getting carsick. But you should have told me earlier, and I could have stopped."

Gail was quite happy for him to go on thinking that that's all it had been, and grasped at his first statement to change the subject.

"I'm afraid Sister Drew hadn't really finished telling me about any of you before you arrived and then there was no time afterwards." Gail wondered silently about that again as she added, "I don't really know any more than the fact that your mother's been in the hospital and you've been responsible for the children while your sister has been away."

He told her briefly about seven-year-old Jacky and her five-year-old brother Robbie, and then added casually, "You must know Aunt Jean well to be prepared to trust her word enough to take us all on, sight unseen."

Or desperate, she thought, but said sharply, "And you must trust her judgment to give me a job without knowing anything about me."

Unexpectedly, he grinned. "Quite a woman is our Aunt Jean. Have you known her long?"

"About four years. And you?"

"Oh, all my life. She was a bridesmaid at Mum and Dad's wedding. We've seen her off and on as long as I can remember, but lost touch not long after her fiancé was killed only a day before their wedd—are you going to be sick again?"

She was staring wildly at him as he half rose to his feet. Her mouth opened, but no words would come. She shook her head and, with a shaking hand, raised her coffee cup to her suddenly dry lips.

"Are you sure?" Jim looked anxiously at her as he subsided again. "You went dreadfully pale again."

"I'm. . .I'll be fine soon," she gasped at last and was grateful when he waited silently for a while until she had sipped more of her hot drink. At last she managed to say huskily, "You said you've known Aunt—Sister Drew all your life?"

He hesitated for a moment and then rubbed his hand briefly over his face and sat back in his chair.

"Oh, yes. She's a marvelous person but was very bitter and unhappy for a long time, though. She really loved her student nurses, especially when she was the tutor sister when they had hospital training. Now she finds it harder, she says, when the students spend so much less time actually in the hospital with the patients and more time at the university. At the time we met up with her again, her whole life revolved around her work and Mum couldn't get over the change in her. But, that was just before she became a Christian and she's just so different, now."

Jim was smiling at some fond memory and didn't appear to notice that Gail sat up a bit straighter and stared at him. She closely watched his reaction as she said, "I heard she'd become very religious during the past two years."

"Religious? I suppose you could call it that. Only I've found that religion and true Christianity are often two entirely different things. Are you a Christian, Gail?"

Jim was smiling gently but, to her annoyance, Gail found it hard to meet the penetrating blueness of his eyes. Before the accident and her stay with Aunt Harriet, she would have blithely said, "Why, yes, of course. Isn't this a Christian country?"

She decided to be blunt. If these people were religious, or whatever he called it, it might be just as well if they knew what she thought from the word go.

"I don't know what I think about God anymore. I certainly don't like what some people seem to be sure He is like. And what's more, I'm not at all interested in finding out either," she finished defiantly.

The blue eyes darkened, and Jim's smile disappeared.

"Are you religious?" As soon as the impulsive words were out, Gail regretted them.

Jim lowered his eyes and toyed with the handle of his cup, and then looked at her and spoke slowly as though he were choosing his words carefully. "No, I wouldn't say I was religious, but I have handed over complete control of my life to Jesus Christ." He ignored her slightly puzzled expression and glanced at his watch, before rising to his feet. "I'm afraid we'll have to get going. Perhaps we can talk about this some other time when we aren't quite so tired."

This time, somehow, getting into the car was all a little easier. After he closed her door, Gail quickly busied herself fastening the seat belt, and she forced herself to look around the interior. The inside was familiar, but the upholstery was a different color, and there was a cassette player in the dashboard as well as a radio.

Then, the car was in motion and Gail felt the waves of tension beginning to reach for her again.

Jim began to talk quickly about Will. He chattered on cheerfully about the fourteen-year-old who was still in high school and then, without waiting for her to respond, rambled on about his mother and life generally on the farm.

Later, Gail remembered very little of what he had said. She guessed that he was using the therapy he handed out to the carsick children. Take the mind off the car's motion and hopefully the stomach will stop churning.

It had been a long, sleepless night at Aunt Harriet's and an even longer and emotionally fraught day. His quiet voice was somehow soothing. It didn't demand any response. It just droned on and on, and gradually faded away.

Several times, Jim glanced at the sleeping woman. Once, her head slipped sideways and, as he steered with one hand and slowed the car, he reached over into the back for a pillow. As he tried to ease the pillow under her head, she opened her eyes for a moment. With her eyes still closed, she took it from him and tucked it under her head and leaned against his shoulder.

"Thank you, darling," she murmured softly, and then was asleep again.

Jim grinned to himself. He rather liked the way she snuggled against him, and wondered who "darling" could be.

Then his forehead creased with thought, as the smile disappeared.

"I think you've sent us a curly one here, Aunt Jean," he mused silently to himself.

At last he shrugged and glanced at the clock on the dashboard. He gripped the steering wheel a little more firmly and pressed his foot down on the accelerator.

Gail jolted awake as the car left the smooth highway. She was dazed and, for a moment, wondered where she was.

"We're nearly there, Gail," a quiet voice said. "Sorry about the rough road."

Gail jerked upright. "Ouch!"

"Stiff? I was afraid of that. You must have been exhausted to sleep so soundly. I've decided to drop you off first and then I'll go over to the Garretts' and pick up the children. What on earth!"

The tired voice sharpened at the same time the car slowed down next to a belt of dark trees. Through their branches Gail saw the outline of a house. Several lights were blazing.

"There shouldn't be anyone here," Jim muttered.

He hit the brakes and the car stopped with a jerk. With a brief "Wait here!" he was out of the car and disappearing among the trees.

Gail stretched, moving her head gingerly. She had never slept like that before in a car. She hoped Jim wasn't too fed up with her. She opened the door and climbed out. A dog not very far away started barking furiously. After peering in its direction, she decided it must be tied up somewhere because it didn't appear, so she moved a few paces away from the car. Suddenly, the barking stopped and the stillness of the night settled around her.

It was a little cool, but not a breath of air stirred the drooping branches of the trees that Gail could now see were pepper trees. A path disappeared amongst them. She hesitated, and decided she had better do as he had told her and stay put. She glanced up. It had been a long time since she had seen stars sparkling so brightly in such a dark sky. City lights always dimmed the stars, she thought regretfully.

A door slammed and footsteps crunched on the path. Gail swung around as the dim figure of a girl came up to the car.

"Miss Brand? Jim sent me to get you." The voice was a little high-pitched and bossy. "He said to come on in and he'd unload the car in a few minutes."

The voice was also cold and unfriendly. Without waiting for Gail to move, the girl spun around and disappeared. Gail reached back into the car for her purse and then hurried after her.

Something must definitely be wrong. The path curved through the trees and then across a lawn badly in need of some attention. It finished at a brightly lit patio.

Gail paused and hesitantly pushed open a screen door that led into a wide, long corridor. A rattle of plates came from a room on her left, so she made her way toward it.

It was a large kitchen and the girl was putting cups and saucers onto the large table in the center. When Gail appeared in the doorway, she paused and carefully looked her up and down. Gail began to bristle at her rudeness until something like dismay flew across the girl's pretty face as she took in Gail's tousled curls, her attractive features, and neat figure.

"You're the woman Jim said had come to help out, but . . .but you're no older than I!" She spat the low words at Gail. "Why on earth did you have to come?"

The words were choked off as footsteps sounded in the

The words were choked off as footsteps sounded in the corridor. She grabbed an electric kettle and turned to fill it as Jim walked into the room.

"Sorry to desert you, Gail. This is Hilda Garrett, a neighbor," he said briefly. Gone was the quiet, relaxed face that had laughed across at her in the restaurant. His eyes were red-rimmed and his expression grim.

"How do you do, Gail? I'm so glad Jim managed to get you at such short notice. How fortunate that you were out of work."

The change in Hilda's face and voice was such a contrast that Gail had a sudden hysterical desire to laugh. The words had been accompanied by a sweet smile that did not light up the venomous, pale blue eyes.

"Hilda brought my mother and the children home." Jim's voice was abrupt and Gail was glad it was Hilda he was scowling at. He continued in a voice dripping with icicles. "What on earth possessed you to go into town with the children and let her persuade you to get the doctor to discharge her today? You know I wanted her in hospital until I had someone to look after things. We'd have been in a fine mess tomorrow if I hadn't been able to bring Gail back with me."

Gail felt a little sorry for the girl who blushed scarlet and said miserably, "Well, I thought that. . .er. . .I could stay a few days, and—"

"Look, Hilda, I thought we'd already discussed that. Your own father needs your help at the moment." Jim bit his lip, as though choking back more words, and then continued in a softer voice, "Oh, well, I guess as it happens it's worked out okay. Let's have that cup of tea and get to around a bit in the morning before you go home."

He turned toward the door and missed the savage look that Hilda flung at Gail.

"But. . .but Jim," she protested angrily, "couldn't I just stay a few—"

"I'm afraid the answer's no, Hilda." Jim paused as another thought struck him. "I suppose you've got your things in Beth's room," he said ungraciously. When Hilda jerked her head speechlessly, he sighed and wiped his open hand over his face. "Sorry, Gail. Afraid you'll have to bunk down in the sleep-out for what's left of the night. I'll get our things out of the car."

There was a grim silence in the kitchen as the screen door slammed behind him. Hilda swung around, but not before Gail saw the tears in her eyes. With her back carefully to Gail, she busied herself with the teapot and then went to a large, built-in cupboard and whipped out a cake tin.

"Look, I'm sorry," began Gail in her pleasant voice, "perhaps we—"

"I don't need your sympathy!" snapped Hilda. "And don't expect any help from me in the morning, either."

"If you could just show me where the sleep-out is, perhaps I could make my bed," Gail tried again after a brief pause.

"You bet you'll make your own bed. But his lordship wants some supper first. I'll show you when I'm ready!"

Gail gave up. There was silence until Jim appeared, laden down with cases, and it was he who showed her to the sleep-out and helped her make up the bed.

When they finally made their way back to the kitchen,

they found it deserted. Gail sensed that Jim shared her relief as he reboiled the kettle. They sat talking easily for a short while. Gail apologized for sleeping all the way. It didn't seem to matter anymore as Jim dismissed it lightly, teasing her gently. Then he chased her off to bed while he turned out the lights.

It had been an exhausting day, but the sleep in the car made it hard for Gail to settle down. She thought of their conversation in the restaurant and suddenly hoped that one day Jim might explain to her what he meant about handing over complete control of his life to Jesus Christ.

She had never heard anyone else talk like that before. In fact, she knew she had never met anyone like Jim before . . .or Hilda for that matter. She grinned into the darkness. She didn't realize until the morning that, as she at last drifted off to sleep, she hadn't once had to deliberately stop herself from thinking of Wayne and her family.

four

"Don't ya think she can wake up now, Jacky?" It was a very loud whisper that penetrated the haze of sleep.

Gail stayed very still as a much softer whisper said "Sssssh! Uncle Jim said we weren't to disturb her."

The very loud whisper dropped a fraction. "But the 'Orror's gone now, and she'll need 'er breakf'st. She must be starved!"

Gail thought it was time to stretch and open her eyes.

"Now look what you've done!"

The soft whisperer sounded worried and then there was the sound of small feet scurrying away. A few moments later, Gail heard a bustle out in the hallway.

"Hang on a minute, I'll push open that door a bit more." Jim's voice was a little anxious. "Watch that jug, Robbie."

A small procession marched into Gail's room.

A dainty, snowy-haired girl carried a breakfast tray up to Gail. An even smaller, fair boy clutched a china jug in two small hands.

"Oh, you darlings!" said Gail.

Jim's lips twitched. Warmth flooded Gail's face.

It had been a long time since Gail's mother had brought her a small tray on her first morning home on holidays and then sat on the bed and chattered away about all the things that interested them both.

Tears pricked at Gail's eyes. She sat up and leaned over the tray to hide them.

47

"We made it ourselves, didn't we Uncle Jim? Only I wanted to cook you an egg, but he thought you might just feel like toast on your first morning," said Jacky.

"An' I made that, too," Robbie piped up.

"Oh, you only buttered it—" began Jacky loftily.

"Now you two, what about we let Gail eat in peace before it gets cold," interrupted Jim as he began to usher them toward the door. He glanced back at her from the doorway and started to say, "You can say hello to—" and then stopped. He hesitated, and then gave her an uncertain smile before following the children, pulling the door firmly behind him.

Gail scrubbed furiously at the tears trickling down her cheeks. Idiot! And she hadn't even thanked them! What on earth must he think of her now? She had been sick, slept all the way home, and now he had seen her blubbering over a breakfast tray.

She swung her legs over the side of the bed and examined the tray. Everything was daintily arranged, including a perfect, pink rosebud.

A glance at her watch made her give a slight gasp. It was horribly late. She ate quickly, wondering about the rest of Robbie's whisper. *Who was the 'Orror?* Then she sat up a little straighter. Hilda! She jumped off the bed and rummaged for her bag. She swallowed the rest of her tea and toast as she rapidly dressed in a pair of slacks and a blouse.

When Gail walked into the kitchen a little later, Jim was washing up and had two small assistants waving tea towels. He turned and gave her a piercing glance that briefly reminded her of that moment in Sister Jean Drew's office. With a gulp, she remembered her deception and hurried into speech.

"Thank you so much for my lovely breakfast," Gail said quickly before anyone could speak. "It's been a long time since I've had such a nice breakfast in bed. . .er. . .like that." Her voice trailed away lamely as she thought of the weeks of hospital trays. She busied herself putting the tray on the table and stacking up the dirty dishes before carrying them over to the sink. "I'm sorry I slept so long. Hello. You must be Jacky and Robbie." She smiled at them, avoiding Jim's face.

They said hello a little shyly and returned to wiping the dishes.

"Well, I'm afraid I wasn't going to let you sleep much longer, as I have to go down to the sheds soon and Mum's still asleep."

"Grandma sleeps and sleeps," remarked Robbie as he dried a plastic cup.

"That's 'cause she's been sick, silly," said Jacky.

"But I wanna tell her about Bennie—"

The small boy stopped abruptly, and his mouth began to quiver as Jacky wailed, "Robbie!"

He glanced up guiltily at his uncle and then grabbed a spoon off the pile of shining wet cutlery just put on the drainer. Jim's hands stilled as Jacky also glanced quickly at him and then applied herself more industriously than ever to polishing the plate in her hand.

"What did you want to tell Grandma, Robbie?" Jim asked very quietly.

Poor Robbie opened his mouth and then snapped it shut. He looked at Jacky and then back up at Jim. Two big tears welled up.

"Perhaps I could finish clearing up in here for you, Jim," said Gail quickly. "And seeing the children made my breakfast, perhaps they could go and play outside for a while."

Jim hesitated. He was frowning and for a moment Gail was afraid he was going to pursue the matter. Then he grabbed a hand towel and wiped his hands dry. His smile at the two children was so unexpectedly gentle that Gail caught her breath.

"Off you go, you villains. But Jacky, don't forget Grandma will get tired very quickly and you mustn't bother her with anything I or Gail can help you with."

As the screen door slammed behind two flying figures, Jim looked at Gail. He sighed. "I don't suppose you know much about little boys and puppies?"

"Puppies?"

"Yes, puppies," he mimicked. "Or I should say, a puppy. If I remember correctly, Bennie was a name selected by Hilda for one of her collie's pups." Jim frowned again. "She offered to give the children one of the pups, but I asked her not to mention it to them for a while. Things have been hectic enough without an untrained puppy running riot."

Gail moved closer and picked up one of the discarded tea towels. "Do you think Hilda might have promised Robbie the puppy?"

"That's more than likely," said Jim a little grimly. "Look, put down that tea towel and come and sit down for a minute. Mum will be awake soon, and I'd better put you in the picture a little."

He pulled out a chair for her, then looked at it in dismay before pushing it disgustedly under the table and pulling out another one. He looked ruefully at Gail as she sat down.

"I'm afraid the peanut butter smeared on that chair brings me to the first couple of things—my mother's health and the state of this house. Did Aunt Jean tell you Mum is an asthmatic?"

"Yes, she did." Gail thought for a moment, and then suddenly heard herself saying, "Look, before we go into that, I'd like to say that as it happens I've had a bit to do with a boy and his puppy. My. . .my brother had one," she finished abruptly and looked down at the tablecloth.

"Oh," he said blankly. "Oh, well then, perhaps you can talk that over with Mum. The poor little kids need something to take their minds off their last disappointment." He rubbed his hand over his face with the gesture that was becoming familiar and Gail saw how drawn and weary he still was. "They're disappointed that I didn't bring their mother home. I tried to keep their minds off that by helping them make the tea and toast." He stopped, a sheepish expression entering his face. "In fact, I. . .I'm sorry, but would you like some more breakfast than that?"

She smiled and shook her head. "No, that was fine, thanks. I loved what you brought in."

She wondered about giving some explanation for the tears, but he grinned and said "That's okay, then. Look, about Mum." He rested his chin on both hands and looked at her consideringly. "I don't suppose you've ever seen anyone in an asthma attack, have you?"

Jim's eyebrows rose slightly as she felt her cheeks grow hot. "Well, yes, as a matter of fact, I have."

"Oh good, that's a relief. At least you mightn't panic as poor Hilda did once and be convinced that she is gasping her last." He looked a bit ashamed when he went on to say, "Sorry, that's a bit hard on her I guess. But those sudden severe attacks were one of the reasons why I was hoping Aunt Jean would have been able to come. Mum's had occasional bouts of asthma the last few years, but since a . . .a family upset earlier this year, she's been getting worse. The doctor refused to discharge her this time unless she had more help at home. I'm doing all I can, but I'm getting more and more behind with my work."

"How was your mother last night?"

"She was exhausted," he said abruptly. "Hilda had no right to take the children in to see her. I was forced to accept her offer to look after them yesterday. I didn't dream she planned to bring Mum home so she would be entrenched here when I returned. She claimed this morning she knew Aunt Jean wouldn't be able to get away on such short notice at this time of the year and—" He stopped short, as though realizing how angry he was starting to sound, and finished in softer tones, "Anyway, she went home early this morning."

The large brown hand moved over his face again. He stared at Gail. She managed to look steadily back at him.

"So, that leaves you. Aunt Jean seemed to think you would be capable of being housekeeper, mother, and nurse, all in one."

"Nurse!"

"Don't tell me that disturbs you the most? I only meant you'll have to keep a close eye on Mum and somehow try to stop her from doing too much again."

"Oh. Oh, I see. What about the mother bit then?"

He looked anxious. "Those poor little scraps are pretty bewildered about the whole business. Did Aunt Jean also tell you about Beth?"

"Beth? The woman you were with in Sydney? No, she didn't mention her. Look, all she said was that your sister's husband had been injured in an accident and, because there had been marriage problems, she didn't want to leave him at all. Isn't that what you meant about not bringing their mother home?"

Jim looked puzzled for a moment, and then his face cleared. "Oh, it sounds like we never mentioned my sister's name. She's Beth," he said simply. "She's just had confirmation from the doctors that her husband's stay in a hospital in Sydney will be longer than they thought. We've been trying to get him transferred to a Brisbane hospital, but they're still too worried about the effect of the trip on him. She's been staying with church people, but we had to find a flat closer to the hospital."

"The poor dear. I didn't dream. . .of course, Beth's room." She saw the look of inquiry on Jim's face and added quickly, "I thought Beth must be your girlfrien—" Jim was grinning madly, and she stopped in confusion, then raised her chin again and spoke with what dignity she could muster. "Last night you said Hilda had her room. I thought you must have gone to Sydney to. . .to. . . . Anyway, that's beside the point," she hastened to add as the grin became a smothered chuckle. "It's a shame Sister Drew didn't tell me your sister was in Sydney. I might have been able to meet her so she would know who was going to help care for her children."

All the amusement drained out of Jim's face. "I doubt we would've had time. It was pretty hectic. She's been under tremendous pressure for the last few weeks. She and her husband were separated. He had his accident some months ago, and she was dreadfully upset because he had refused to let anyone contact her until recently. He was involved in a dreadful accident in the Blue Mountains."

Jim paused as they heard a soft footstep in the hallway. He didn't notice the sudden drawn-in breath of his companion as he sprang to his feet.

"Hello, you must be Gail."

Gail stood up as Mrs. Stevens entered the kitchen. She put her hand in the soft, thin hand extended towards her. A faded version of Jim's clear, searching blue eyes studied her from a pale face framed by softly curling, graying hair. She looked thin and frail, as had many chronic asthmatics Gail had seen over the years, and was obviously glad to sink down onto the chair Jim had been using. She must have been awake for a while after all as she was dressed in an attractive cotton frock.

Jim scolded her gently. "Mum, you should have stayed in bed today."

"Not on your sweet life," she interrupted him cheerfully. "I've spent days and days in a wretched bed. I want to get to know Gail. Why don't you go and see how Will is getting on and leave us to start doing that very thing."

Jim hesitated, and then smiled a little ruefully at Gail. "I don't know how you're going to do it, but do try and stop her from starting the spring cleaning or something equally as strenuous. I guess Will does need help."

He bent and kissed his mother on her cheek. Her frail hand came up and touched his face. With a pang, Gail saw the look of affection that passed between them.

Well, at least he didn't let that screen door slam quite so hard, Gail thought as she and Mrs. Stevens looked at each other in silence.

"Yes, they do rather let that door slam," Mrs. Stevens said. She gave a low chuckle at the look on Gail's face. "I guessed the children had been banished when I heard that door before."

"Yes, they're outside somewhere. Perhaps I should check on them?"

"No, no, they'll be with Will down at the machinery shed. Perhaps you could put the kettle on though, and make us a pot of tea instead."

As Gail filled the electric kettle and switched it on, she decided it best to confess straight away.

"Look, Mrs. Stevens, I'm afraid I can't cook very well."

The older woman chuckled, and said in a relieved voice, "Well, that's a relief." She saw Gail's look of astonishment and laughed outright. "If you knew what I've had to put up with these past few weeks from someone trying to convince me she was a paragon of all the virtues, you'd know what a relief it is to have someone who will admit she can't cook!" She suddenly looked a little contrite and added quickly, "But that's not very kind. It's just that I'm so relieved Jean sent you."

Her voice and manner were so friendly and warm that Gail felt some deep inner coldness and reserve begin to dissolve. It didn't take long to make the tea and toast. Gail opted for a cup of coffee, and soon they were chattering away as though they had known each other much longer than just a few minutes.

As they talked, Gail began to realize what a strain Mrs. Stevens had been under. She was much younger than Gail had thought she would be and, although she didn't say so outright, the task of looking after her own two sons as well as the two children had become just too much for her after her recurring asthma attacks. Jim had at first been able to help a great deal, but the harvest was only a few weeks off. He was too busy now on the property to spend much time in the house. Mrs. Stevens's face glowed as she talked about her eldest son.

"He's been absolutely marvelous. God's been so good to me, giving me such a son. Since his father died when Will was only eight, he's tried so hard to fill the gap that that loss meant to us all." Her face clouded and she sighed. "I suppose you know about Beth and Arthur? She changed so much after they were married, and even more after he left her. She'd been drifting along, and that really shook her up. And now—"

The screen door slammed, and a tall gangly boy with a mop of unruly dark auburn hair appeared in the doorway. "Hi, Mum! Sure good to have you home!"

"It's sure good to be home," Mrs. Stevens said fervently. "Will, have you said hello to Gail yet? Why Gail, what—"

Gail had sprung to her feet. She felt dizzy and disorientated.

He was the same height. His voice was the same—uneven, cracking a little. And that unruly auburn hair...the freckles. . . .

"Will, did you say? But his name's Bill," she croaked in a dazed voice.

The boy gave a self-conscious laugh. "Well, it's really William, but Dad's name was Bill, so they've always called me. . ."

His voice wavered again on some of the same deep notes as that other fourteen-year-old had. Gail sank back into her chair and, with a low moan of anguish, covered her face with both hands.

Mrs. Stevens went into action. "Will, how many times have I told you to wash yourself in the laundry first before coming into the house after you've been in the shed."

She winked at him and jerked her head significantly towards the door. He disappeared fast. Then she went to Gail and laid her hand on the bowed shoulder.

"You mistook him for someone else, dear."

Gail knew she had made a fool of herself, but couldn't find her voice. She felt gentle fingers soothing her, and at last took her hands from her face and looked up.

Mrs. Stevens's kind face changed as she saw the ravaged features.

"I thought he was Bill. My. . .my young brother." Gail closed her eyes tightly for a moment and, for the first time, forced herself to put the dreadful knowledge into words.

"He. . .he. . .was. . .was killed. Car accident." She opened her eyes and again fought for control at the horrified expression on Mrs. Stevens's face. "Your son. He's uncannily like him. Especially his voice. I. . .I never gave a thought to how old your other son might be."

"I'm so very sorry, my dear. Will was a most unexpected gift from the Lord rather late in our marriage. He goes on the bus to high school during the week and that doesn't leave much time for him at home. He's a tremendous help to Jim on the weekends." The gentle voice went on quietly, allowing Gail time to recover, while at the same time busy hands started stacking their dirty cups and plates. "Look, I'd rather welcome the chance to putter around in here for a while if you think you could start on the bedrooms, Gail. And then I can help you get lunch."

Gail thankfully escaped. She worked swiftly, using the defense mechanism she had tried to perfect at Aunt Harriet's. Busy hands and feet forced her to concentrate on the task at hand and protected her emotions from utter chaos.

By the time she had transferred her things to the bedroom next to the kitchen, she was feeling calmer and began tidying the children's room. As she went to put away some clothes in a drawer of the dressing table, she noticed a small plastic container with some holes in the lid. Her tight lips relaxed when she lifted the lid. She hesitated for a moment, took one glance around the now tidy room, and carefully carried the container back to the kitchen.

"Mrs. Stevens, what do you think I should—" she paused as Will turned and looked uncertainly at her. A knife thrust shook her for a moment, but the distress on his face made her force a smile at him and hurriedly say, "The children weren't the only ones to occupy their room last night. Look."

With a relieved expression Will approached her and peered into the container. He chuckled. "Hey, Mum, Robbie's collecting snails again."

"Oh, he's a positive menace with his creepy crawlies.

Do take the wretched things out to the back patio please, son. I suppose we should be thankful they aren't spiders!"

Gail shuddered as Will disappeared. "That's one thing I have a real thing about. Them and snakes."

"Well, I'm afraid at times we have both. Do be careful near any long grass, Gail. The children are pretty good now at watching out for them. Jim killed a large brown snake on the back patio a few weeks ago."

"They don't come into the house, do they?"

"Well, we've never had one in this house, but it isn't unknown on the Downs."

The rest of the morning passed quickly. Gail unpacked her cases as quickly as she could, only pausing to sit on the bed when she pulled out the bundle wrapped in an old towel at the very bottom of the last case. She hesitated and then lovingly cradled it in her hands. At last she reluctantly unwrapped the two photo frames with their precious contents. Pain ripped through every cell in her body as she looked down at the smiling faces.

It was still too soon. Time heals, people had told her. But how long does it take, her heart cried in anguish? With shaking hands, she placed them face down under a pile of winter jumpers.

Perhaps by next winter, she thought bitterly as she walked quickly from the room.

There was only one thing about the rooms in the lovely old house that struck the wrong chord with Gail. As she moved from room to room, she was disappointed as she realized that these people must be as religious as Aunt Harriet. The religious pictures and texts were not as ostentatiously displayed, but each room held at least one.

On her own bedroom table a daintily framed painting told her that "Prayer changes things." The largest painting of all hung above the bed she figured must be Jim's.

Aunt Harriet had a painting of the head of Christ prominently displayed in her lounge room. It had portrayed Him as a gentle, Anglo-Saxon type. Gail stood for several moments before the one in Jim's room. This was a man's Man. The features were strong and rugged. The face was deeply tanned with dark hair blowing in the wind. There were beads of sweat on His forehead. And those eyes. . . .

Gail turned from it with an impatient shrug and a frown. Her eye caught a small plaque on the dressing table. It pleaded, "Please be patient. God hasn't finished with me yet."

She glanced back up at the painting before thoughtfully making her way back to the kitchen. Well, at least these people may not think they had all the answers.

When she entered the kitchen, she saw with dismay that the table was set and lunch preparations were well underway. Mrs. Stevens was sitting down, talking to Jim as he sliced some cold meat. Abruptly, they stopped their quiet conversation when they saw her, and her head unconsciously went up.

"Oh, I'm sorry. It took me longer than I thought."

Jim grinned at her. "Not to worry. I've been doing this for quite some weeks now. I didn't intend for you to start today anyway. Perhaps you could call the children and supervise their hands."

Lunch was a cheerful affair. Afterward, the kitchen was tidied in record time so Gail could be taken on a tour of the farm. When this had been suggested during the meal, she had tentatively mentioned she should really start on the huge pile of washing. This had been greeted with disappointed cries from Jacky and Robbie. Mrs. Stevens stated she intended to have a sleep while they were all out. Jim had said decisively that after putting up with chaos so long, one more day was neither here nor there. So she gave in.

Gail was very relieved their transport was a rather battered utility and not the Holden and, when their first stop was the huge machinery shed, she found herself enjoying Will as he took it upon himself to point out to Gail the various machines essential for operating a successful grain farm.

She heard in rapid succession about the monster harvesters, called "headers" on the Downs, the huge bulk bins that would be fitted onto the semitrailer truck, the large tractor, combines and rakes, the sunder-cuts or "disc ploughs" as some people apparently called them. As Jim at last steered them back to the utility, Will was still explaining carefully to a bemused Gail that the large cylinders, called "rollers," had to be used some years to press the soil down onto the planted grain. When they eventually scrambled back into the ute, Gail's head was whirling with a mass of farming lore.

Jim started to laugh a little as he let in the clutch. "Sorry about that, Gail. We don't expect you to remember all that in one sitting—or even three! Afraid when you live here all your life you take it a bit for granted. You'll get used to all the new words and ways gradually."

She nodded and smiled ruefully. "It did all come a bit fast and furious."

They had driven away from the sheds down a bumpy track that led around the fence of a paddock filled with golden, waving wheat. No hill or rise obstructed her view across miles and miles of plains.

"There aren't any trees," Gail noticed. "Has it always been like this or did the early farmers clear them all away?"

"There are miles and miles of treeless, black soil plains here. There's only a few patches of scrub, mainly around the Condamine River and its branches farther west. The farmers never had to clear anything except prickly pear cactus."

"I think I remember my. . .my dad saying something about that once. Didn't some insect have to be imported to get rid of it?"

"Aussies are peculiar people," Jim mused. "Most of the pests we have, whether animal or vegetable, have been deliberately brought here. The prickly pear was brought in, and by 1925 had covered over thirty million acres. Then, the government had to bring in a moth from South America to let its larvae eat it out. The old-timers reckon they couldn't ride a horse across the plains once for the pear. Its sharp cactus points would rip a horse to pieces. It was all grazing land then of course, but wasn't even much good for cattle in large areas. Now, most farms only have house cows and concentrate on grain crops, although more and more are turning to cotton when they can get the underground water to irrigate."

Gail could see a faint smudge on the horizon toward the east, and an even fainter, lower one toward the west. She was too polite to say so, but she had always thought flat country looked monotonous. But she looked with new eyes at the waving wheat on each side of them. It was all rather beautiful. The only green patches followed the few fences, and even they were few and far between. It was vast, and perhaps a little intimidating for someone who had only known the rolling hills around the fruit-growing areas where she had been raised.

When they had traveled a couple of kilometers from the sheds, Jim pointed out a distant clump of trees around some buildings. "That's the Garretts' place. Hilda's dad is a fine man. Her mother died a few years ago and there's only the two of them now. His faith in God hasn't faltered at all. If you'd like to come to church with us on Sunday, you'll probably meet him. Look! There's a snake!"

Gail was just in time to see the flash of sun on the long shiny reptile as it whipped across the rough track into the wheat.

She shivered. "Your mother said you killed one on the patio. Do you have a lot of them?"

She was glad to have a chance to prevent him from saying more about religion. For a moment she wondered what she was going to do if they expected her to go along to church with them.

No way, she thought.

"Not really," Jim answered her and then commented, "If this hot weather holds, it should only be another couple of weeks and we can start harvesting. Grain's not hard enough yet," he explained in answer to Gail's questioning look. "I'm glad, too. We've got a lot of work to catch up on beforehand. You'll be extra busy then, Gail."

"I like being busy. But perhaps you'd better tell me what to expect."

This Jim did for the rest of the drive across the paddocks. He explained that he had to hire men to drive the trucks and they would need to be fed. She would have to do all the running to and from school with the children until the summer holidays started in a few weeks' time, shop for supplies, and do a variety of things that could come up.

There was no further opportunity to talk about religion. Gail had been wondering if she should tell him straight out about her aversion to going to church with them. As it happened, after tea that evening, she was glad nothing more was said. She would certainly have been more embarrassed than she was before.

Everyone had finished their meal and she began to gather the dirty plates. Robbie said reprovingly, "Aren't we 'avin' our readin'?"

Gail had briefly wondered why the two children had not raced off the moment they had finished eating. She had put it down to just good training, but now she paused and looked inquiringly at Jim.

He stood up and took a book down from the top of a cupboard. He hesitated for a moment and then said quietly to Gail, "We always try and have a brief Bible reading and prayer after tea every night. We'd love you to share it with us, but if you'd rather not—"

"Uncle Jim!" Jacky sounded scandalized. "Of course she's going to share! You made us to start with and now it's right up to an exciting bit she won't want to miss. We missed our reading last night at the Garretts'."

Gail looked down helplessly at Jacky's indignant face.

She put down the pile of plates and meekly sat down in her place again. She was looking at the precariously piled plates and missed the glance Jim and his mother exchanged. At her barely perceptible nod, Jim sat down also and opened the Bible.

"Right," he said cheerfully, "what were we up to Robbie?"

The small face frowned in thought for a moment, and then lit up. "The boy was just loadin' 'is shanghai, and the giant was comin'."

"It's the story of David and Goliath, silly," Jacky said importantly.

It was a very long time since Gail had been told this story by an enthusiastic Sunday school teacher. It had been a long time since she had bowed her head and listened to such a simple, but sincere prayer. But never before had anyone included her by name in their prayer, as, with a start, she realized Jim was doing.

". . .and please be with Gail and help her as she gets to know us and we get to know her. Amen."

Later that night, Gail lay staring into the darkness thinking again of Jim's prayer. She felt confused. With these people, their religion seemed such a natural part of their everyday life. Mention of God or faith seemed to crop up very regularly in their conversations.

In comparison, her Aunt Harriet's religion was forced, kept for Sunday observances and special meetings. From Jim's attitude over the Bible reading, she knew she only needed to say she didn't want to go to church and nothing would be said. Perversely, she wondered if she should go and see how their church services compared.

She was still wondering about it all when she fell asleep.

five

On Sunday, Mrs. Stevens decided she still was not strong enough to venture out to church. Gail happily grasped the excuse to stay home with her. By the time they all returned, Gail and Marian, as she insisted Gail call her, had thoroughly enjoyed a cooking lesson and established an easy rapport.

The days sped by as Gail attacked the neglected household tasks. Most nights she fell exhausted into bed with the comfortable feeling of having worked well, and slept deeply.

Jim was very busy preparing the machinery for the quickly approaching harvest but, one afternoon, Gail heard him call out to her a moment after the screen door slammed behind him.

She answered him, but her smile faded as she looked up from her never ending ironing and saw the unusual look of determination on his face.

"Right, it's time for you to come with me to pick up the children," he said.

"But I've still got all this. . . ." Gail faltered to a stop and felt a tremor pass through her as his eyes hardened.

"You've no choice, I'm afraid, Gail. I have to be sure you know where to go and that you can drive in any emergency. It's essential on a farm."

His tone was quite gentle, but she knew he would be

inflexible on this as she knew with a sinking heart that he was right. Reluctantly, she switched off the iron.

He simply turned and headed toward the back door. Slowly, she followed him as he disappeared through the pepper trees. By the time she reached the driveway, he was waiting for her beside the old utility.

"I'm afraid we'll be a bit cramped for room as I don't let the children in the back when we're out on the road," he said carelessly as she felt the relief flow through her. "There's the bread, milk, and mail to fit in, too."

To Gail's horror, he opened the driver's door and gave a mock bow. "After you, madam."

"Oh!" she said blankly.

Blue and brown eyes locked.

"You do have a license, don't you?"

"Yes, of course. But I—"

"In you get, then. I'd rather you practiced with me as a passenger than with the kids."

The firm set of his mouth, and the equally firm hand under her elbow, gave her no option. Before she knew it, she was sitting behind the steering wheel staring at it. The door banged closed beside her and, a moment later, the passenger door also was closed decisively.

"Better do up your seat belt first," Jim said blandly.

Her eyes flew to meet his now expressionless ones. Somehow he knew that her sickness after leaving the airport had been more than simple motion sickness. She fumbled with the seat belt.

"Haven't you ever driven a utility before?"

"Yes. But I—"

"Was it so different from this old bomb?"

Gail took a deep breath. She turned her head to tell him she would not—could not—drive this or any other vehicle.

"Yes, of course you can drive this old ute," he said crisply before she could even open her mouth. "And the Holden, too!" he added for good measure.

Suddenly, a surge of anger swept through Gail. How dare he ignore her feelings about this! Both small, capable hands hit at the steering wheel.

"You do need keys, though."

There was a distinct drawl in the soft voice. Gail snatched the dangling bunch of keys from him and their fingers touched for a brief moment. Then one large, strong brown hand gently held hers while one finger touched one of the keys.

"Ignition key."

How dare he! Her hand was trembling so much that it took a moment to push the key into the ignition and turn it until the motor caught. They jolted forward a couple of paces and the motor died.

"It has a clutch," the soft drawl reminded her.

She gritted her teeth, shoved a foot firmly down on the clutch, and turned on the motor again. She worked the pedals and they jerked forward a little unevenly. But they were moving. Gail gripped the wheel tighter and tried to dodge the potholes, but seemed to succeed in hitting every one. By the time she had driven onto the main road, she was still tense, but had stopped trembling.

"Atta girl!" The soft drawl had a smile in it this time.

Gail glared at him after she had changed fairly smoothly up into top gear, and they were rattling along at a reasonable pace. There wasn't a flicker of a smile on his face as he gazed at the road ahead. She refused to speak to him. There wasn't even any need to give her directions, she fumed. The road was long and straight and led to another wider road that was also without a curve as it disappeared into the hazy distance.

When they arrived, the bus was already there. Jim jumped out, called greetings toward another couple of drivers of large sedan cars, and quickly bustled the three youngsters to the utility.

"Something wrong with the Holden, Jim?" she heard Will ask as he climbed into the back.

She didn't hear Jim's reply but, as she suddenly realized he had come in the utility for her sake, she felt her anger drain away. He could have insisted she drive the Holden.

With Jacky and Robbie squashed in between them on the return trip, chattering about their day, Gail was forced to break her silence. She made suitable comments in the right places, but never once glanced at Jim again. They stopped at the small shelter near the property's front entrance to collect the bread and milk delivered by the mailman and, by the time they reached the house, Gail was beginning to feel very foolish and embarrassed. How stupid Jim must think she is.

After the others had climbed eagerly out of the vehicle, she just sat anchored behind the steering wheel, staring blindly through the windscreen until her door was at last wrenched open.

"Are you all right?"

There was a wealth of concern now in his crisp tones. She didn't look at him, just nodded her head once.

"I'm sorry, Gail. I had to know you could drive. Some

days I may not be here, and if ever anyone became sick and needed to be taken to the doctor. . . ."

At last, she turned her head and looked at him. Jim smiled at her. It was a very beautiful smile. There was concern, even admiration for her courage in it. But what caught at some hidden part of Gail's heart was the wealth of gentleness lighting up his dark face.

"Good, Gail. You'll do," he said softly, and then leaned right into that dirty old utility and kissed her.

Jim had disappeared along the track to the house before Gail at last moved. She slowly climbed down from the cab of the utility and, for a moment, leaned against it for support. Her legs were a little shaky. Whether it was because of the fact that she had actually driven again or because of that soft, tender kiss, she wasn't quite sure. Her fingers rested on her lips. It had been the merest butterfly of a kiss, right on the mouth.

At last she straightened and started toward the house. Gradually, her steps became more buoyant. After all, Jim had bullied her in his own subtle way. It had only been a gesture to express his apology. And she had actually driven again!

Why then did she go crimson when she reached the kitchen and Jim turned and smiled very gently at her?

In the days that followed, Gail was only too thankful to be able to drive again. Jim was so busy she took over the grocery shopping as well as the school run.

And then the three children came down with chicken

pox. Poor Jacky had a sudden, raging fever and had to be fetched all the way from school. The boys were not as sick initially, but all three needed a lot of time and patience until they were allowed back at school. Beth called often and Gail's heart went out to this mother so far away.

And not only Beth rang. The friendly farming community inundated them with offers of help, including one of the young male schoolteachers Gail met the day she had picked up Jacky. One day, while she was finishing off the kitchen curtains, he even asked her for a date, which she politely refused. Will had answered the phone, but when she turned after hanging up, Jim was standing behind her. Her chin lifted a little as she realized he must have heard part of the conversation. She didn't have a clue why he was frowning at her.

"That was Tony," she said, and added quickly as his eyebrow tilted, "Tony Blair, Jacky's schoolteacher."

"Oh, that Tony," said Jim blandly, and then added a little nastily, "A nice enough young fellow, I've found. Asking after his pupil, I suppose?"

Gail was annoyed with herself as she felt her cheeks getting hot for no apparent reason. She nodded rather abruptly and moved past him into the kitchen. Jim followed her. He looked around at the clean walls and cupboard doors. The vinyl chairs no longer dared to have peanut butter or vegemite sticking on them.

"Very nice," he observed.

Gail was still feeling annoyed. She wasn't quite sure if it was with herself, with Tony, or with him. A couple of curtains were still waiting to be threaded back on the rods and, without answering, she walked over and picked them up.

"Gail, I hope you feel free to accept any invitations you might receive," Jim drawled softly.

She swung around just in time to see him rub his hand over his face. Before she could speak, he spoke again.

"You haven't had a day off, in fact, since you arrived." The drawl in the deep tones was even more pronounced and there was a very thoughtful look on his face.

"Oh, it hasn't seemed like an ordinary job at all," she said impulsively. "It's been more like sharing the life and work of a family. I. . .I mean—"

She broke off, suddenly feeling very embarrassed. After all, she was not a member of the family. She was still just an employee and she had known them for only a very short time. He must think her very presumptuous.

Jim had not said a word. He was so still that at last she ventured a glance at him. She stared.

He was beaming from ear to ear. "Why, Gail," he said with a warmth that lit a glow in Gail's lonely heart. "That's the nicest compliment I've heard for a long, long time."

They were still smiling at each other when Will burst into the kitchen.

"Got a date, yet, Gail?" he said breezily.

Gail did not notice that the smile was wiped off Jim's face in a flash as she turned to Will.

"I just might have, young fellow me lad," she said lightly, still grinning widely.

"Don't ask personal questions, Will."

Jim's words were so stern, and the words said with such

a snap, that Gail and poor Will gaped at him.

He scowled at them both, turned abruptly, and marched out of the kitchen.

The children had been back at school only a couple of days when Jim arrived home with the mail as usual and handed two bulky letters to Gail, several to his mother, and retired to read his own in peace. With a slight shock, Gail noted that both of the envelopes had Miss G. Brand typed neatly on the front as Sister Jean Drew had arranged.

The first envelope contained a letter from Ann Green. She was delighted, and eagerly tore it open. Ann wrote as she talked, and told all the latest news about her obstetric training, concluding her letter with an appeal to Gail to write to her and let her know why she had disappeared off into the blue the way she had.

Gail sighed as she put the letter down. Ann's hospital talk was like the echo of a past life in which, Gail suddenly realized, she had lost a lot of interest. It was a relief to be away from the wards full of sick and even dying people. She was enjoying home life so much with the Stevenses. They had so quickly accepted her as one of themselves and, as she thought of the noise and frantic life of the city of Sydney, she felt a great yearning to be able to stay on. No one had mentioned any time when they would no longer need her, but she guessed it would not be until well after the harvest had finished. Jim thought they should be able to start fairly soon. Then it would take about three weeks, if all went well, and finish just before Christmas, he had told her.

Gail picked up the other envelope. Two letters fell out, one looking official enough to be an account. Then she saw her lawyer's name printed on the back. She stared at it, and then slowly and reluctantly opened the envelope.

It contained information about the legal winding up of her father's estate and the sale of her old home. It also told her the date in the future for the coroner's inquest into the accident. As she read it through slowly, it brought with it the smell and the reminder of the small office she had visited a couple of times since her discharge from hospital. Worse than ever, it reminded her afresh of all she had lost.

Her eyes were dry and burning, her throat aching. Why had this come today when for the first time she had begun to feel she might at last be able to find a new tomorrow? She threw it down, and grasped hold of the other letter.

This one was from Sister Jean Drew. She read it through quickly, and then stared blindly into space. So even this haven was threatened. What should she do? She slowly read several parts again. There was no doubt it had been written only after a great deal of careful thought. It seemed that Sister Drew's main concern was that she had persuaded Gail to change her name, but there was something else about the letter Gail couldn't quite put her finger on, and she began to feel more and more uneasy as she read.

"You see, my dear," Sister Drew had written, "I'm afraid I'm far too impulsive. I still have so much to learn about letting God control my life—and my lips. And so I have put you in what I realize is a position of deceit. I've become more and more convinced that God would never want one of his children to use deceit as we have, even with the best of motives. So I think you should talk to Marian at least.

"Have they told you about Beth's husband yet? I'm sure they would have, and so I guess by this time you know the rest of my plan as well. I hope you can forgive me if I have caused you more hurt. I did so want you to live in a loving Christian home for a while.

"Do please let me know as soon as you can how you've been getting on. Perhaps Marian and Jim know already. I sincerely hope so."

She concluded her letter by urging Gail to let her know if ever there was anything at all she could do for her. And then she added, "My dear, I know you have lost all those who loved you deeply. I want to tell you that over these past few months, you have become very, very dear to me. You have been constantly in my prayers. Oh, how I long for you to have that close relationship with God through Jesus Christ. He alone can fill your life with meaning and purpose again."

As Gail read her final words over and over, the tears were at last released and streamed down her cheeks. The hard knot in her throat gradually eased.

Sister Drew had signed herself as "Your loving friend."

Once before she had mentioned to Gail that the only One Who could really help her was Jesus Christ. Lying in her hospital bed of pain and bitter loss, she had barely listened then. Now, although worried about the future, she felt warmed by the love that reached out to her from the pages of the letter. Gail supposed that the plan she mentioned might be something to do with this "becoming a Christian" business.

But what should she do?

She knew very well by now the high standards Jim and his mother lived by. They would probably despise her. She couldn't lose their respect and friendship now. Where would she go? Back to the once earnestly desired haven of a lonely room in the Nurses' Home?

She shuddered.

Here, she was part of a family again. Inevitably, the Stevenses would have to know.

But not just yet, her lonely heart cried. Not just yet.

The rest of that day she drove herself ceaselessly. She thought of all the reasons why it was best not to say anything for a while. She would probably have to leave once they knew. They needed her help too much, until at least the harvest, she tried to convince herself.

Gail went to her room early that night, telling Jim she had a headache, which was perfectly true by then. She missed the sharp, intense look he gave her as she dejectedly left. But several times during the evening, Gail had caught Marian staring at her with a strange expression on her face. She had also been very quiet for most of the day.

She must know something's upset me, thought Gail, and almost panicked at the possibility of facing awkward questions.

It was a relief to lie staring into the darkness, away from that searching glance. She so much dreaded the questions that would have to be answered when she told them her real name. She couldn't even allow herself to think about the accident, let alone talk about it. *Even to Jim,* she thought for no real reason before tossing and turning for what seemed hours.

There was something tight around her. Holding her down. She couldn't get away. She couldn't breathe.

And someone was screaming. . .over and over. . . .

"No! No! No! Leave me alone! Let me go. They're burning. . .burning. . . ."

It was dark. So dreadfully dark. She couldn't move.

Then hands were holding her firmly. Warm, comforting hands. Strong hands. There was a beam of light, a tender voice. She stopped struggling and felt herself lifted and held against something warm with a steady throb. Crooning, soothing words reached out to her.

"Hush now, Gail, dear. It's all right. Only a bad dream. Wake up now. . . ."

Gradually, the dreadful moaning and shuddering eased. At last she stirred and reluctantly moved away from her secure haven.

"Jim?" she whispered hoarsely.

"Yes, it's only me. You were calling out, and I came," he murmured simply.

She felt the warmth of his arms leave her as she sank back on her pillow and stared up at him. He had switched on the bedside lamp. It's light shone on his pale, anxious face. As she looked at him, slow tears began to trickle down her cheeks. She threw up one hand and covered her eyes. She felt his warm fingers close gently around her other hand.

"I haven't had that nightmare for such a long time," she managed at last. "I can never remember what it's about. Only I'm so scared when I wake up."

Jim remained sitting silently on the side of her bed, just holding her hand until she stirred again with a deep, shuddering sigh.

"Would you like to talk about it?"

She froze.

"No," she replied at last in a frightened whisper, and pulled her hand away from his warmth.

"Would. . .would you like me to make you a hot drink, or just an aspirin—"

Gail abruptly interrupted his low, hesitant words. "Just an aspirin would be fine."

He brought her the medicine with some water to drink.

"I'll be okay, now. Thanks, Jim," she felt compelled to say to him while he stood silently beside her.

She slid down in the bed and turned her head away as though she couldn't bear to have him see her tear-stained face.

"Gail, you know you're going to have to talk to someone about what's troubling you." She didn't move, and she heard him sigh, and then felt the brush of his lips on her forehead. "Just call if you need anything," he said very softly, and then he was gone.

Gail lay in a tense huddle until faint light crept through the window and at last she dozed off.

They all overslept. There was such a rush to take the children to catch their school bus that no comment was made about dark circles under two pairs of eyes.

Gail retreated into herself; Jim made no attempt to break through the barrier of averted eyes and compressed lips.

In the days that followed, he never referred to that night

even though Gail drove herself mercilessly. She was vaguely aware that he and his mother anxiously watched over her. They both made a few attempts to get her to slow down. She tried to smile and even made a weak joke about employers usually urging their workers to do more work, while hers tried to stop her. Marian had looked hurt and Jim had just scowled and walked away.

After that, Gail made a determined effort to be bright. She knew by the look on Marian's face that she was fooling no one. The tension in the house increased until even the children began to eye her warily. Before, they had accepted her freely and easily into the pattern of their lives as only young children can.

It couldn't have lasted, Gail acknowledged much later. The day it all blew up had been a particularly hot one. Despite the heat, Gail had still insisted on doing some more baking to finish filling the freezer before the harvest commenced. Marian had stayed in the hot kitchen and helped her, despite all of Gail's arguments. They prepared a cool salad for the evening meal. By then, Marian's face was white and drawn.

Straight after tea, Jim packed his mother off to bed. Will raced off with some friends who picked him up each Friday to take him to the youth fellowship meeting at the church hall. The children were told to do their homework by such a stern Uncle Jim that they went into the lounge room without a single protest and watched a favorite movie on television.

Gail apprehensively glanced at Jim as he strode back into the kitchen and picked up a tea towel to help her with the dishes.

"You know, there was nothing I could do," said Gail anxiously. It was the first time she had ever seen him really angry. "Your mother just ignored me. She organized us both in the kitchen and insisted on racing around."

"Righto, righto! I get the message!" Controlled anger seethed in the deep voice. He remained silent until Gail reached down into the cupboard for something to scour the saucepans. Then he exploded.

"Oh no you don't!" Jim flung down his towel. He snatched the pan from Gail as she began to vigourously scrub it.

"That wretched thing is clean of food and can do without a polish tonight! Gail! You don't know when you've had enough. But I do!" he roared. "You're not going to do another thing now. You're going into the lounge room to put your feet up and relax. You can watch television, or read, or even talk to me—or go to bed for all I care! But you're not washing one more teaspoon tonight! Or mending another school shirt! Or sewing on another button! Or helping Jacky with her homework! Or. . .or any other thing you can dream up!"

While he roared, brown hands whipped plates away into cupboards at a furious rate. Doors slammed shut. Blue eyes flashed with fire. As he finished the tirade, he grabbed Gail's arm, and began to bundle her out of the kitchen.

They were almost to the door when, to Gail's absolute horror, she felt the tears of exhaustion and hurt at his anger well up and a small sob escaped.

Gail felt hot with embarrassment when she thought about it later. But then, it seemed the most natural thing in the world to rest her aching head on his shoulder when he sighed at her and drew her to himself.

Then, Jim put both of his strong arms right around her. It was the same comfort she had known the time of the nightmare. It was bliss. It was peace. She relaxed completely against his solid warmth. The tears trickled down her ashen cheeks. She felt his breath stir her hair. For a moment, he seemed to envelope her even closer into himself and then his arms relaxed. She felt a large handkerchief begin to mop up her wet cheeks, and only then did she fight for self-control and move away from him.

Jim pulled out a chair, and gently sat her down. He turned away to fetch a glass of water and, when he returned, placed it on the table near her before he, too, sat down. He frowned down at his clasped hands resting on the table and was very still as she picked up the glass and sipped from it.

He certainly knows the value of silence, Gail found herself thinking as at last she raised her head and looked at him.

"I'm sorry, Gail. I shouldn't have spoken like that, especially when you're so tired."

He rubbed his hand over his face with the gesture that Gail suddenly recognized, with a little shock, had become not only very familiar but very dear to her since that first time in Sister Drew's office.

"You're very tired, too," she said huskily after a pause.

"Yes," he said briefly. "All this work on the machinery should have been finished ages ago. It's nearly done now. Another few hours tomorrow should do it." He stopped, and after a moment said slowly, "Gail, you've been driving yourself too hard. Perhaps you don't realize it, but you're making it all even harder on Mum. And me."

Her lips opened to protest, and he added quickly, "No, don't say anything. Let me finish. Mum hasn't said anything, but I know that her overdoing it today was her own way of trying to help you not do so much. She's very worried about you." His voice dropped, and he said very softly, "We both are, Gail."

Gail's head drooped down as she continued the battle to control herself. She gritted her teeth as the pressure mounted.

"I didn't bring you here to slave like this. Some of the house could have waited—"

"No, no!" Gail burst out. With a sense of helplessness she heard herself say, "You don't understand! I've got to keep busy. I can sleep at night then. I don't have to lie awake in bed. I don't have time to. . .to remember. . . ."

The last words were barely audible as her head went down on the table. Sobs—deep wrenching sobs—started to rip through the frail body.

At first Jim sat as though stunned—these were more than tired tears. They came from some deep hidden well and showed the depth of the pain that was tearing her to pieces.

"Dear God, help her," he choked, and was half out of his chair when she raised her head.

"I'm. . .I'm. . .sorry. . .I'm. . .so. . .," she gasped between sobs.

As she rose, shaking violently, Jim was beside her. She shrank from his touch, shook her head, and blindly groped toward the doorway.

"The. . .the children. . .I'll be all right. . .I. . . ." She moved out into the hallway and added softly, hopelessly, "Somehow. . .have to be. . . ."

Jim let her go. As she stumbled to her room, she was vaguely grateful that he had not tried to stop her. Some grief was too poignant, too private, for any audience.

Once safely in her room, she fell across the bed. The sobs were moans of anguish. Tears that had been stifled so many times flowed like a fountain bursting out of an irrepressible spring.

Gradually, the storm subsided. The physical and mental strain of the past few days took their toll, and she fell into a deep, deep sleep.

The exhausted woman did not hear the hushed voices of Jacky and Robbie as Jim put them to bed. He answered their anxious questions as best he could, helping them to say their prayers for poor Gail who had been crying because of some very sad things that had happened to her.

Will came home late and found the screen door tied back so he wouldn't forget and let it slam. An exhausted Jim came out of the lounge room cautioning him to silence, briefly explaining.

Several times, Jim had crept to Gail's door and listened intently. Once or twice he nearly went in to her while she was still sobbing. Will had been in bed for some time when Jim went to listen once more. His knock was very soft before he opened the door and crept across the room. Light from the open doorway fell on the curled up Gail on the bed.

He stood there for a while, rigidly watching her even breathing, with only the very occasional catch of breath from the storm of tears. Then large, calloused, but tender hands finally moved to slip off her shoes and ease her beneath the blankets.

He yielded to the temptation to kiss her very gently on the lips he had so briefly touched once before. Her deep sigh made the tall figure straighten and freeze as she rolled onto her side. In the dim light, he saw her lips tilt in a smile. She murmured something he couldn't catch, and she snuggled deeper into her pillow as a child does when she knows she is secure and loved.

The man's heart was breaking as he stumbled into his own bedroom, onto his knees beside his bed, and cried out to the One Who had never failed him.

six

The slam of the screen door woke Gail the next morning. She stirred and stretched luxuriously. Then she stilled as she remembered the previous night. Her eyes felt sticky and her throat dry. She frowned, trying to remember if she had removed her shoes, and was sure she had not. And someone must have pulled back the blankets and covered her. She glanced at her watch and sat bolt upright. As she began to scramble from the bed there was a brief knock on the door.

"It's only me," Jim's voice called.

The memory of his warmth and comforting arms brought a confused blush to her face. What a spectacle she had made of herself!

"Come on, Gail, you sleepyhead. It's late."

Gail tried to straighten her badly crumpled dress before calling reluctantly to him to come in.

Jim grinned at her as though it was the most natural thing in the world to sleep all night in daytime clothes. With a flourish, he placed a tray across her knees, stepped back, and gave a mock bow. "Your servant, madam!"

Gail looked anywhere but at his face. She felt the tide of red spreading wildly across her face.

"And I did cook you an egg this time, and I cooked the toast, and I buttered it, too. So make sure you eat every crumb. And hurry up. We're going on a picnic."

He shot the last words at her as he went out the door.

She looked at the daintily arranged tray. It was the same as her first morning except for the boiled egg. This time, the rosebud was red and even its thorns had been broken off.

When every crumb was gone, she quickly pulled out her clothes for the day and raced to the bathroom for a quick shower.

Marian was buttering several slices of bread when Gail carried her tray into the kitchen. Without giving her a chance to murmur the apology trembling on her lips, Marian said briskly, "Hello, my dear. I'm glad you've had a good rest. Now, if you'd like to rescue those boiling eggs on the stove and mash them, we'll finish making these sandwiches. I've packed some cake, fruit, and drinks. I think that's all we need for our picnic."

Gail quickly did as she was asked, relieved that no explanation was apparently necessary, and said slowly, "I thought Jim still had some work to do on the header?"

"Jim laid down the law this morning. No more work today. We're going to the river for a swim and a picnic. About time, too. We've all been working far too hard without a break."

The older woman's voice was filled with gentle compassion, and Gail raised her head and looked at her miserably. Marian hesitated for a moment, and then put her hands on Gail's shoulders and looked into the dark brown eyes, bright with unshed tears.

"My dear, Jim told me about last night. He feels very ashamed at upsetting you. We've become very fond of you in the short time you've been here, Gail. We know that something tragic has happened to you in the past. Whenever you feel able to, we'd count it a privilege to share your suffering. Talking a little about it may help you, too."

Gail swallowed, managed a brief nod, and then reached out and gave Marian a quick hug, kissed her on the cheek, and moved back to the table, not trusting herself to speak.

"Now, if you've finished with those eggs, I'll slap them on this bread and you could go out to the laundry and bring in the cooler. Then, we might be ready when they come up from the sheds."

Marian's brisk words sounded very like her son at his bossiest and, when a slightly bemused Gail returned, Marian was cutting the sandwiches as though her life depended on it.

"Bathing suits," Marian said rapidly. "Just thought of them. I do hope Beth packed the children's, otherwise they'll have to wear an old pair of shorts. Do go through their drawers, Gail, and grab a few towels out of the linen cupboard. I hope you have a suit?"

"No. Sorry, afraid that's something I didn't buy."

As Gail raced out of the room, she thought of the shopping spree Aunt Harriet had taken her on to replace all her clothes destroyed by the fire that had raged through the wrecked car. Suddenly, she was amazed to realize it was the first time the unbidden memory had lost most of its jabbing pain.

It was a scramble to get ready and there was no time left for dwelling on other things. The children were excited and in everyone's way until Jim banished them to the back seat while the adults finished loading the car.

Gail had caught some of the children's excitement, and

never gave a thought to the green Holden into which they were packing the picnic gear. At the last moment, she raced inside for some forgotten travel rugs and, when she returned, breathlessly accepted the seat in the front as Jim held the door open for her. She was busy passing the rugs over to Marian as the car went into motion. As she turned around and automatically grabbed for her seat belt, she stilled. Robbie was bouncing up and down in the center of the wide front seat. Across the top of his head her glance caught Jim's very serious expression.

"Okay?" he queried softly.

She took a deep breath, and suddenly it was all right. "I'm fine."

His answering smile reminded her vividly and unexpectedly of that soft kiss in the utility. Color flooded her cheeks and she quickly turned away. She missed the way Jim's smile changed to a broad grin of sheer amusement.

The car was eventually parked under some tall river gum trees on the bank of a gently flowing river. As they all scrambled from the car, a flock of pink and gray galahs rose with a screech. Only Jim's roar stopped the children from rushing down the grassy slope to the water.

"Jacky and Robbie! No one goes near the water until the car's unloaded, you're in your suits, and I'm ready, too! Come here you terrors and spread out this blanket for your grandmother."

Reluctantly, the children helped the adults set up the gear. Then, Will took off his clothing under which were his swimming briefs, while Gail helped two wriggling young ones do the same thing.

"Come on, Uncle Jim," they chorused impatiently as he

appeared in his swimming trunks. They cheered, poised for flight. Jim quirked one eyebrow at Gail.

"Sorry," she laughed, "no swimming suit."

"Well, you can jolly well come for a paddle. Roll up those trousers and let's put these three out of their misery."

Gail hesitated, and glanced at Marian.

"Go on, off you go, dear. I might wander down later."

As they raced off, Will took a hand of each child. Jim reached out and grabbed Gail's hand and pulled her after them. Neither saw Marian's rather startled look at her son.

"Come on. I've got to make sure there are no unexpected hazards," said Jim.

"Hazards?" she gasped breathlessly as she tried to keep up with his long strides. His strong hand gripped hers tightly as they scrambled down the steep slope to the water's edge, and then let her go as they caught up to the others.

"Deep holes, logs washed down, even broken glass sometimes. Have to be careful with rivers, and we haven't been here since last summer."

Apparently, the children were used to this first inspection of the waterhole for safety. They sat on a ledge and dangled their legs in the water while Will and Jim waded in and swam and dived for a few minutes.

"The water gets pretty deep over there." Jim pointed a few meters downstream. "So stay up at this end and you'll be safer."

Robbie let out an Indian warwhoop and jumped in. Gail sprang back, but some of the water splashed on her.

"Robbie, you beast!" wailed Jacky as she wiped some water from her eyes. "Wait for me!"

Gail was delighted to see they both could swim quite well. She sat down on a grassy outcrop and slipped her feet into the cool water. After a brief swim, Jim came back and hauled himself out and perched on a log near her. Suddenly, she felt self-conscious. Except for that brief moment in her room, this was the first time they had been alone since the previous night, and she wondered how she could apologize for her breakdown.

Jim sat watching the antics of Will with the two squealing children. The silence became a little strained.

"Jim, about last night. . .," she at last blurted out.

He turned his head. His face had lost all its twinkle and sadness filled his eyes. "You don't have to worry about that, Gail," he said quietly.

Suddenly, it became important to make him understand. She heard her own voice saying, "But I'd like you to know why. . .why I was upset. Why I've been so silly. . .working so hard."

The blue eyes went very dark. He turned his gaze back to the swimmers. "You don't have to if it upsets you too much. But sometimes it does help to talk it out." He hesitated, and then continued slowly. "Mum told me your brother was killed in a car accident. You limp sometimes at the end of a long day. Although I think not as much as when you first arrived." He paused again. "Were you driving the car?"

The soft query shook her. How dreadful if she had been! She swallowed hard.

"No," she said softly at last, "my father was driving."

He stiffened, but was silent. She took a deep breath and closed her eyes.

"I was the only survivor."

Even as the whispered words escaped, she realized for the first time that this was what haunted her the most. She felt guilty for still being alive.

Jim bit off a soft exclamation and, when she opened her eyes, he was watching her. There was no condemnation there, only compassion, and some other expression she could not quite make out.

Will and the children had moved closer to them. As he stood up, Jim reached out and pulled Gail to her feet.

"Let's go for a walk," he muttered.

He released her while they slipped their thongs back on, and then led the way with brisk strides along a track that followed the river bank until it curved out of sight of the waterhole.

Gail wished he would grab for her hand again. There had been something comforting and strengthening about that firm grip. Even when the track suddenly led up a steep incline, he did not touch her. He stood at the top and waited for her, staring down at the river that was flowing gently below the high bank at this point.

"Do you think you could tell me about it?" he asked softly at last. "Sometimes it helps." He carefully refrained from looking at her as he continued. "There were others in the car?"

She stood silent and still, trying to find the right words, the right place to start.

At last Jim turned abruptly and she saw him swallow as he looked at her. His eyes lingered on her hair, her face, as though he were seeing them for the first time. Then his blue eyes were probing and searching out the very secrets of her innermost being.

She had the absurd thought for a moment that his hands had begun to lift to reach out and gather her to him, but he only moved them behind his back as he leaned against the trunk of a river gum.

Her eyes jerked away from him. And then the words were there. Jim stood like a statue as they began to stumble out.

"Mum and Dad and Bill had come down for my graduation from nursing school." Gail did not see the startled look on Jim's face. "We were on the way home. Wayne. . .," her voice choked.

She swallowed painfully, and turned her head and looked at him. His eyes were filled with pain. She licked her dry lips and forced herself to answer his unspoken question.

"Wayne. . .he was my fiancé."

Later, Gail was to remember the look of desolation that flashed into Jim's eyes with wonder.

"Was?"

"Yes."

Jim turned and moved along the track; his hands were clenched fists. Gail slowly followed him. It had helped to say their names out loud. Suddenly, she wanted to tell Jim about it all. It had been bottled up for too long.

Jim at last stopped and sat on the ground, using the trunk of a tree for a backrest. As he looked up at Gail, his tight lips hinted at his stern self-control. He invitingly patted the ground near him and she slipped down beside him. This time, he did reach out and take her hand gently. Then, he waited.

"The...the car was exactly the same color and model as yours," she began softly, and felt his hand tighten for a moment.

Once started, the words flowed out in a torrent. With them, fled the last of the tension built up over those long, weary months. He listened quietly, except for an occasional soft question. She still could not remember the lead up to the actual smash, or her brief bouts of consciousness she had been told that she had had before coming to in the hospital. Jim shared her anguish as she told him of those first dreadful days of trying to cope with the realization that they had all been killed.

He was angry when she told him about that last confrontation with Aunt Harriet. But, not once did she mention the still-hospitalized driver of the truck, except to briefly state that he was "only injured."

"So you're one of Aunt Jean's girls as she calls you," Jim mused as she at last fell silent.

Gail caught her breath. She hadn't mentioned her last visit to Sister Drew's office. She knew now she would have to tell him her real name. It didn't really matter anymore. Perhaps he wouldn't think too badly of her now that he knew what had prompted it.

"Well, I didn't want to talk about any of this," she began slowly. "Jim, there's something else. Your Aunt Jean—"

"Jim! Mum says it's lunch time!" Will was waving to them from a short distance away.

Jim waved back. "Coming." He scrambled to his feet and looked ruefully at his grass- and dirt-covered swimmers. "I'll have to wash these off before lunch," he said ruefully. "Come on, let's run. We can finish talking another time."

Gail hung back for a moment. "Jim, I'd rather you didn't mention this to anyone, not even your mother. She has enough to worry about with Beth and I—"

"I won't mention a word."

His eyes flashed with a strange expression, and Gail received a jolt as she had the sudden absurd feeling that Will's waiting figure was preventing Jim from reaching out to her. He turned away abruptly with a smile that didn't reach his eyes. "We'd better hurry up or they'll have eaten all the food."

Marian looked intently at Gail when she arrived a little breathless after having run nearly all the way.

"Jim sat in the dirt in his wet togs and is washing it off."

Gail felt the color pour into her face at the suddenly quizzical expression in Marian's eyes, and hid her face as she busied herself getting out the cups and drinks from the cooler.

They were all hungry and set to demolish the huge pile of food. As she ate, Gail was feeling almost lightheaded with relief at being able to talk as she had to Jim. She wasn't even worried anymore about that ridiculous name change business. Later, Jim had said.

After lunch, Jim and Will insisted on taking the children for a wander along the river bank.

"You two women make sure you try and have a sleep while it's quiet," was Jim's parting remark as he made to follow the others.

The two women grinned at each other and, as Jim

walked away, two loud snores obediently came from the reclining figures on the rugs. Through her half-closed eyelids, Gail saw him pull a face at them before racing off with a smile.

Marian and Gail opened one eye each as the silence descended around them again except for the warble of a couple of magpies nearby. Marian sat up and cautiously looked around, and then they laughed at each other and relaxed again on the rugs. There was a comfortable silence.

Gail rolled onto her back and looked up through the gnarled branches of the old gum tree. The two black and white magpies flew up through the topmost leaves.

Just as well they are friendly today, she thought idly.

Briefly she remembered another picnic when she was a child. A magpie had swooped down and viciously pecked at her head. It had repeated its attacks until her parents had at last packed up and moved to another part of the park.

Gail closed her eyes. A tear slid out and slipped slowly down her cheek. She knew it was not just a tear for the past, but because she had at last actually been able to let herself dwell on a bittersweet memory. There was still the ache and the sense of loss, but the sheer agony had gone. Deliberately, she recalled other picnics. Wayne had only taken her once. He had claimed that he didn't like to share his food with the flies and the ants. That picnic had always stood out as a dismal failure, and the first time they had ever had a serious argument.

Gail thought of Jim. She had never met a man who showed such sensitivity and understanding of her needs. He was wonderful with the children. With wonder, she realized there was an integrity and quiet strength about him that she had never before seen in a man, not even Wayne. Many times she had sat quietly, listening to the exchanges between the three Stevenses. They all hated deception and double-dealing of any kind. And yet, she now recognized, they never really hated the people who behaved differently from their standards. They said what they thought to folk like Hilda, but always were kindly in their attitudes toward them.

"You awake, Gail?" Marian whispered softly.

Gail rolled onto her side and smiled at her. "You're not doing what you were told, either?"

"No." Marian's voice sounded husky.

Gail pushed herself up on one elbow so she could see the older woman's face better. "Are you all right?"

"Oh, yes," Marian answered. "I just didn't want to lie here thinking any longer."

Her voice cracked on the last word. Gail saw her teeth grip her bottom lip before she flung an arm up across her eyes.

"Would you like another cup of coffee? I think there's some hot water still in the thermos," Gail said gently after a few moments when her companion hadn't moved or spoken again.

No, thanks, Gail." She turned on her side suddenly to face Gail. "I've been feeling a bit down since getting Beth's letter yesterday."

Letters from Jim's sister had arrived regularly for the children and their grandmother but their contents were rarely mentioned. She had felt it a little strange that neither of the children ever spoke about their father except to automatically ask God to "bless Daddy" in their prayers.

Gail had never seemed to get around to asking how long they expected her to stay or how the sick man was progressing. She knew how remiss she had been, and felt ashamed.

"How is your son-in-law, Marian? Somehow I've never had the chance to ask before," she said apologetically.

"He's not showing any improvement at all. Beth said in this last letter that he has withdrawn right into himself and hardly ever talks, even to her. Before this he was a very difficult patient. The doctors say that the. . .the accident is preying on his mind. Beth wants Jim to fly down again. And that's what's worrying me."

The older woman sat up and rested her chin on her knees, avoiding Gail's eyes.

"I haven't told Jim about that part of the letter, and I'm not sure if I should or not. He has spent so much time and money on trips to Sydney recently. The harvest gets underway next week, and he has so much on his mind. I've been lying here praying for wisdom. Jim has been the only one who seems to be able to get through to Arthur."

She hesitated, about to speak again, when Gail quickly asked the question that had crossed her mind several times. Until now she had never felt free to ask.

"What are his actual injuries, Marian?"

She raised her head and looked steadily at Gail. "The first few weeks they had to concentrate on second degree burns on his back and legs. He also had a spinal injury. Has no one ever told you that he's paralyzed from the waist down?"

She waited tensely for Gail's answer.

"Oh, no!" Gail was appalled. Several things fell into place. This alone explained his protracted stay in the hospital, and Beth's determination to be near him. She stared silently at Marian, who was watching her intently with a strange expression.

"You see, Gail, there's someone who should go and see him." She spoke very slowly and with a peculiar intonation. She hesitated as Gail began to feel rather mystified. "This. . .this person should assure him that the accident wasn't his fault. The courts haven't cleared him yet, but—"

"Are you girls talking instead of sleeping?"

Jim was striding toward them with a mock scowl creasing his face.

It seemed to Gail that Marian took a moment to recover and find her voice before finally saying with a forced laugh, "Oh, dear. Gail, we've been sprung."

Although her voice was determinedly cheerful, she was still on the receiving end of one of Jim's quick penetrating glances. He stood with his hands on his hips, legs astride. He shook his head at his mother.

"Sprung? What kind of word is that, may I ask, Mrs. Stevens?"

"Will's talk, young man—and yours, too, unless my ears have deceived me a few times." She reached out her hands and he hauled her up. "Ouch! I'm stiff. And I like talking to Gail, you bossy bully. She's my kind of person." She smiled gently at Gail as she scrambled to her feet. Before Jim could retort, she whipped up the rug and began shaking the grass and dirt from it as she continued swiftly, "Gail, if you'd like to stretch your legs and chase those other children away from that patch of sand, this bossy old thing can start packing all the stuff away in the car."

Gail laughed at the slight emphasis on the word "other." Jim's lips were smiling, but he eyed her steadily before she turned away. As she disappeared down the bank, they heard her gaily call out. Mother and son looked at each other.

"She's a lovely girl, Jim," she said softly. He nodded abruptly, and she added hesitantly. "Jim, dear." She stopped, and took a deep breath. "Do be careful, though. I'm afraid there could be a hard streak in her and I don't want you to be hurt."

"Mum!"

Jim's disapproving exclamation of utter amazement was heard by Gail as she came swiftly back to them. She wondered briefly at the slight constraint they showed toward each other as she helped them pack up and she wished she had had a chance to find out more about what was happening in this delightful family.

The sun was almost at the horizon and the cool air flowing into the car lifted Gail's curls as they sped home. Jacky had triumphed over her brother and now sat between Jim and Gail.

Robbie chattered away in the back to his grandmother about the great dam they had been building in the river, but Jim was very silent, letting Gail respond to Jacky's conversation. She found herself watching him a few times.

Jacky's head at last drooped onto Gail's shoulder, and Marian told Robbie to be quiet while Jacky had a rest. Soon, a peaceful silence reigned. Gail was almost asleep herself when Robbie began softly humming a tune. Will soon picked up the melody and began to sing the words. Gail listened lazily as Jim joined in. Then she realized they were singing about a deer panting for the water like the soul panted for the Lord. It was a haunting melody and Gail strained to hear the words as she stared blindly out the window at the golden paddocks of wheat already being harvested in some places.

One song led to another. Marian joined in a couple of times and it became obvious to Gail that this was a regular feature of car trips. Even the sleepy children even suggested a favorite or two. Gail recognized some of the tunes from her own far-off days at church. Once, she even ventured to hum the melody of one whose words she had forgotten.

Jim must have heard, but didn't glance at her. The next song he chose was an old, very well known hymn, "What a Friend We Have in Jesus."

They all sang it enthusiastically. Gail ventured to softly murmur a few words until suddenly the meaning of what she was singing stung her. She stopped abruptly.

She was not sure if she had ever taken anything "to the Lord in prayer." By these people's standards, she certainly had plenty of reason to pray. And she wasn't quite as sure any more that all religion was a waste of time. It certainly seemed to work for people like Jim and his mother.

Gail did not realize just how the daily evening readings from the Bible had subtly begun to influence her. The stories of the ancient heroes told in the first part of the Bible had been replaced by stories of Jesus Christ. Quite a few times, Gail had stood and stared at the painting over Jim's bed and wondered. She had gradually become used to hearing herself mentioned specifically in the prayers. It no longer embarrassed her. Instead, she felt warmed and included in the family circle.

The sun had at last slipped below the distant horizon, and it was all so peaceful that Gail was sorry when the car slowed down and swung into the long driveway. Through the dusk, she could see the top of the red corrugated iron roof peeping above the clump of pepper trees.

Gail's heart gave a sudden leap at the sense of home-coming. This place and these people were becoming very familiar and dear to her. She felt a tinge of fear. Loving people could hurt too much. Suddenly, she wondered if she should stay much longer.

But as the car pulled up beside the house, she turned and looked across at Jim as he glanced at her. He smiled gently, and she caught her breath.

She could not leave, yet.

Not yet, her treacherous heart pleaded. Not yet.

seven

Sunday morning breakfast was well underway by the time
Jim entered the kitchen. A rather embarrassed Gail glanced
up at him as he said his usual cheerful "good mornings"
and poured himself a cup of tea.

"You have to hurry this morning, Uncle Jim," said Jacky
importantly. "We're all helping because Auntie Gail's
coming to church, too."

Gail was busy making toast and didn't see the look of
delight that flashed across Jim's face. His mother did. She
frowned suddenly.

"Now, who told her it was my turn to preach?" Jim
sounded severe, and Gail swung around quickly.

She saw the grin on his face and said stupidly, "Why, no
one. I. . .I just thought it was time. I. . .I mean. . . ." She
took a deep breath and turned to rescue the toast. "I didn't
even know you did preach. Don't you have a minister?"

"Oh, yes," piped up Robbie. "Only he's boring and they
don't have him every week."

Gail stared, and then smiled weakly as Marian and Jim
chuckled. Will roared. Jacky, however, was scandalized.

"Robbie! What a thing to say! It's just because Uncle
Jim is ours that he's better!"

The children looked curiously at the convulsed quartet.
Jacky's bottom lip began to tremble. A dark tide of red had

darkened Jim's tanned face. His mother came to the rescue.

"Stop! Gail won't know whether to come to church or not." Her eyes twinkling merrily, she went on to explain. "Mr. Telford is the minister in Toowoomba who comes and takes the services as often as he can. Otherwise, a few of the members are rostered. Now, come on, finish your breakfast. We're all making our own beds, too, and then it'll be time to go."

The church was a small weather-board building in the corner of a paddock not far from the huge grain silos next to the railway line. Trees and shrubs had been planted around the grounds and the grass was neatly trimmed. It gave the general impression of a place well-used but lovingly looked after.

A group of people were standing, talking on the path near the front steps. They called friendly greetings and Marian quickly introduced Gail to the group as a whole.

"Everyone, this is Gail Brand, who has been helping us out. Please tell her your names after the service because we'd better go in now."

That name thing again, thought Gail as she responded a little shyly to the chorus of "hellos."

How she wished she had been able to speak to Jim alone after they had arrived home the night before. She had gone to bed wondering if he was avoiding her by going off to his room so early. Common sense told her now that it had probably been to finish preparing for the service. She frowned. There had still been something this morning. She thought they had been so close on the river bank, and now he seemed to have retreated.

The inside of the building was as unpretentious as its outward appearance. It was bright with bowls of attractively arranged flowers and the sunshine that streamed through the open windows. As they filed in, a slight, gray-haired man was playing softly on the small electronic organ. A hush and stillness gradually descended on the people. Even the row of young children in the front settled down. A table on the platform was covered with a white throwover and, after a few moments, Jim came through a door at the side and moved quietly to sit on the chair behind it.

During the service that followed, Gail couldn't help making continual comparisons between the simplicity and sincerity of these people with the pomp and ceremony of that other service with Aunt Harriet. Perhaps both types of services were needed by both types of people to draw them to worship. If that were the case, these farmers and their families were her kind of people. Later, she was a little surprised to learn that about half of the congregation that morning were employed in many occupations. Even the local Bush Nurse had been there.

Gail was ashamed afterwards to realize how her mind had wandered during Jim's sermon after the simple communion service. To start with, she had listened intently, as he spoke with a deep conviction about the importance of knowing Jesus Christ. Jim urged them all to open their Bibles regularly and read and study it that the Holy Spirit could show them Jesus Christ. The idea of Christ's being the one theme of the whole Bible was a new one to Gail. In fact, a good deal of what Jim said she had never remembered hearing before, and she found she couldn't really understand some of it.

As the moments passed, Gail found herself dwelling more on the speaker than on the message. He was wearing the same suit she had seen him in that first time in Sister Drew's office. His face was alight with belief in the truth of the words he was using to convince and encourage his listeners.

What a fine man he is, she thought dreamily. *He not only tells other people to do these things but he does them himself.*

She had often seen his Bible left open on his desk beside other study books. One morning, she had been a little early doing the bedrooms, and his mother had stopped her from going into Jim and Will's room. Jim was running late and would probably still be having what she had called his "devotional time," she had explained matter of factly. Perhaps this was another one of the reasons their religion seemed to be so different from Aunt Harriet's. Never once had she seen a Bible in that cold house except carried in the hand to church.

After the service, the conversation seemed to be mainly about the harvest, about bags and bushels of wheat per acre, and the never ending topic of the weather.

"Why, hello, Gail. How are you surviving?"

Gail swung around to face an unsmiling Hilda Garrett. Her own polite smile faded at the hostility she could see in Hilda's face.

"So glad the Stevenses talked you into coming to church at last. Or did you come because Jim was preaching?"

The venom in the low tones made Gail's cheeks burn. Her chin tilted, but before she could answer, she realized

Marian had broken off what she was saying to turn and slip a hand inside Gail's elbow. She gave it a little warning squeeze. Gail glanced at her as Marian gave a light laugh. The faded blue eyes glinted at Hilda.

"Oh, dear, Hilda. Don't make me feel any worse than I do. I'm afraid Gail had to ask if she could come this morning because we neglected to ask her. I think she nearly changed her mind when she found out Jim was preaching." She adroitly changed the subject. "And how are those puppies of yours? Gail says she used to have a dog herself when her father owned a farm. So we think perhaps we might be able to have one for Robbie after all."

Gail felt warmed, protected, and suddenly very much an accepted member of the Stevens family. She wasn't aware that Jim had joined them until his deep voice came from behind her.

"Mum, you villain, have you been conspiring against me?"

He rested his hand casually on Gail's shoulder, and cocked an eyebrow at her. She hoped he couldn't feel her trembling. He looked annoyed and, for a moment, she thought he might be angry with her for obviously having mentioned the pup to his mother. Then his hand tightened on her shoulder and she knew he, too, must have heard Hilda's spiteful words.

She forced herself to smile up at him. "We think the pair of us could handle one small boy and his puppy."

"Why don't you come over this afternoon, Jim, and pick it up," Hilda said a little too quickly.

Jim shook his head decisively, "No, Hilda. I'm afraid I have to finish overhauling the header this afternoon. It

would be best if Gail drove Mum and the children over
after lunch."

"You're working this afternoon?" Disbelief rang in
Hilda's voice. "But you never do that on Sunday."

"I never work if it means missing out on church activities," Jim corrected her. "Yesterday, something cropped
up and I didn't get it finished."

Gail looked at him, and opened her mouth to speak, but
Marian slipped in smoothly with "We'd better get moving,
Jim. Gail, would you mind calling the children for me,
please?"

When they were at last on their way home, Gail turned
to Jim and said quietly, "Jim, I'm sorry you had to leave
that work yesterday. We could have gone another day."

He looked gravely back at her. "No, I'm so very glad we
...we...." Very quickly he turned his head away and, after
a brief pause, continued more cheerfully, "We all needed
that break. I can quite easily finish this afternoon. God
knows how important that picnic was and He under-
stands." He hesitated again, and then added slowly, "I try
to keep Sunday as the one day in the week different from
the others because it's common sense that we need one day
of rest. It's not because I believe Sunday is any holier than
any other day in a week lived in His presence."

Gail was silent and thoughtful for the rest of the short trip
home. That had just about explained the difference between Aunt Harriet and Jim. Her religion was something
to be observed on Sundays and all her activities the rest of
the week were more for her own gratification than
anything else. Jim lived every day as though in God's

continual presence. His God did not seem too impressed, either, with outward show. Yet, Jim's intimate relationship with God dictated his very lifestyle.

When she drove up to the Garrett house that afternoon, Gail couldn't help feeling apprehensive about Hilda. However, the man who had been playing the organ that morning came out to the car and was introduced to her as Mr. Garrett.

"I'm sorry I didn't get a chance to speak to you this morning, Gail. Welcome to the Plains." As he took her hand, his face crinkled into laughter lines at her surprised look. "I should have said 'Darling Downs' you reckon? The old-timers often call this the Plains—the black soil plains."

The children had said their greetings and raced off to a shed beside the house where there was a chorus of yappings.

"I'm afraid Hilda had a couple of things to do inside. Why don't you join her, Gail, while we follow the children."

Gail only hesitated briefly before smiling brightly to ease Marian's sudden frown and moving towards the house.

The sullen greeting from Hilda was not very encouraging, but after a carefully worded question from Gail, Hilda began telling her about Polly, the puppies' mother, and her successes at local dog shows as she continued with her preparations for afternoon tea.

When Gail showed how impressed she was, Hilda suddenly beamed and pulled out a drawer full of show ribbons and photographs. As she went on preparing a plate of home-cooked biscuits and as Gail examined the contents of the drawer, Hilda explained some of the various points that the judges looked for.

"I'd love to breed and sell collies." Her busy hands stilled for a moment, and then she added in a slightly louder voice, "When Jim and I are married, I'm hoping I'll eventually be able to go in for them in a big way."

"Married!" Gail felt a wave of devastation and shock hit her.

Hilda put a hand up to her face, and her eyes opened wide. "Oh, dear, I shouldn't have said that," she said in a rush, a rather peculiar look of pleading in her eyes. "It. . .it's a secret. Please, Gail, forget that I said that."

Gail felt bewildered. "I don't understand," she managed through suddenly dry lips. "Are you and Jim engaged?"

Hilda hesitated. The shrieking whistle blew on the electric kettle as it began to boil. As she poured the water into the teapot, her face was hidden from Gail's searching gaze as she spoke very quickly.

"Well, nothing is official you see. With. . .with Beth's troubles and then his mother. . .well, you see nothing can be said, yet. But Jim and I. . . . Please don't tell Jim I said anything, Gail. He'd be very annoyed." She swung around and there was apprehension and fear in her watchful eyes.

Gail swallowed, but her strained voice made Hilda's eyes narrow. "Of course. I'm sure I wish you all the best and I hope—"

When her father came into the kitchen, Hilda thankfully broke off her stumbling words.

The rest of the visit passed for Gail in something of a haze. She didn't see the sharp look Mrs. Stevens gave her and the frown that creased her forehead as she looked thoughtfully at the hectic flush on Hilda's cheeks and her slightly agitated chatter as she served them their afternoon tea.

On the way home, Gail had to force herself not to think about her reactions to Hilda and Jim's plans to marry, and tried to concentrate on the children's excited talk about the puppy, Bonnie.

Gail was helping the children get ready for bed when Jim at last came in for his late tea. It had been hard to wrench the children away from their new pet and Jim was watching television by the time they were settled.

He looked up and smiled at her when she paused in the doorway. It wasn't his usual relaxed grin. To Gail's watchful eyes it held that hint of reserve she had noticed the evening before. Unexpected pain knifed through her.

"Finished at last? Are you going to watch television for a while? I think Mum has headed for bed."

Gail suddenly knew there was no way she could bear to be alone with him just now.

She yawned widely. "I think your mother has the right idea, Jim. Good night."

She thought a look of relief flashed across his face as he murmured goodnight before turning back to the television. As she showered and prepared for bed, she could no longer stop her mind from dwelling on what Hilda had said. When the light was out and she was staring into the darkness, she recognized at last what her reactions had really been to the news that Jim and Hilda would marry. There had been searing agony and savage jealousy.

She began to tremble, curling up in the bed, clutching

the sheet to her tightly.

No. It couldn't be. She mustn't be. Love was pain and grief and sheer hell.

Wayne. Tears trembled on her closed eyelashes. She had loved him dearly. Perhaps in a sense she always would. There was no way she could compare him with Jim. He seemed only a boy compared to the man who had been the mainstay and support of his mother and family for so many years.

And she herself was no longer that same young girl who had so happily planned a future with Wayne. As she thought of him now, she realized it was without the same depth of agony and loss that had enveloped her only a few weeks before. Now, she admitted that was only possible because Jim had begun to fill that special, empty place in her heart.

Suddenly, she sat up and turned on the bed light. Opening the drawer jerkily, she pulled out the photographs. With trembling hands she unwrapped them. She studied the happy family group. Tears blurred her vision. She brushed them away impatiently. Always there would be this sense of loss, but she knew with an overwhelming feeling of relief that she could at last accept that they were gone.

She caressed the edge of the frame for a moment, and then reached over and stood it carefully on her bedside table. Then, she turned her attention to the engagement photo of herself and Wayne. Her smiling, excited face looked plump and girlish, and Wayne seemed so much younger than she remembered. She arranged it beside the other and thought of the last time she had looked at them.

Winter was a long way off, spring had leapt into summer, and now she at last could look at the faces of her loved ones and know that the sadness in her heart would lessen as time passed.

"Only because my heart is daring to love again, my darlings," she whispered softly.

She lay back on her pillow and thought long and deeply about Hilda and Jim. She went over every word, every tone of voice that Jim and his mother had used when mentioning Hilda. There had certainly been anger, but perhaps it had been more like affectionate exasperation with someone they had known all her life. The more she dwelt on Jim's attitude to Hilda though, the more bewildered she felt. There had never been the least sign of any love between them that she could remember. Gail's heart lightened a little. Perhaps it had all been a figment of the poor woman's imagination. She would somehow ask Jim despite the promise made to Hilda. There was no need to let Jim know it had been Hilda herself who had mentioned their relationship.

She must have dozed off with the light on, she realized later when a persistent yapping roused her. Her eyes blinked open and the first thing she saw was the smiling faces in the photographs. She smiled sleepily back at them, then was suddenly wide awake. Bonnie was whimpering for her mother.

Gail jumped out of bed, quickly put on her bathrobe over her nightgown, and ran out into the corridor—and straight into a tall, solid figure!

"Oomph! Where's the fire?" said Jim's voice as he

grabbed at her to stop her from falling.

"Oh, I'm so sorry," she gasped. "It's the puppy. I was afraid she'd wake everyone up."

"That's where I was heading, too. Only I haven't been to sleep yet. Come on, there he goes again."

"She."

Jim didn't pause in his stride as they hastened towards the pitiful sounds now getting more and more frenzied.

"What do you mean?"

Gail wished he would stop holding her arm. All she could think of was the warmth running straight through her like an electricity charge.

"Gail, what did you mean—she?"

"Oh," she gave a nervous giggle as she realized she had forgotten her instinctive correction. "I'm afraid we were misled about the dog. He's a she and called Bonnie, not Bennie."

With relief, she felt him release her as he reached up to switch on the patio light. "On, no! Beth will want to shoot me as it is. She'll just love having all the problems that go with a female dog around the place. Thanks, Hilda!"

Well, that certainly didn't sound like a man in love!

Gail's heart was doing all kinds of peculiar things as they entered the laundry and were greeted with a rapturous welcome from Bonnie. She bent to pick her up, but Jim stopped her.

"Please, don't make too much of a fuss over her or she'll demand us all night. Look in that cupboard for a hot water bottle, please, Gail. I think Mum keeps an old one in there."

They stayed, trying to settle the pup down, until at last

a thoroughly exasperated Jim said, "We're wasting our time—and our sleep. Every time we make for the door, she starts again. I'm afraid we're just going to have to leave her."

She looked up at him rather pleadingly but, before she could say anything, he creased his forehead fiercely, but his eyes twinkled at her as he said firmly, "And no, he can't go to sleep in your room, or he'll end up on Robbie's bed and then my dear sister will certainly murder us both!"

He ushered her to the door and turned the laundry light off as he added, "Let's just hope she doesn't do this for too many nights in a row."

He pulled the door closed as Gail went ahead of him down the path. The light from the patio was cut off by the corner of the laundry and the ground was only dimly lit for a few paces.

As Gail went to take a step, something slithered quickly across the path. She screamed and jumped back, bumping into Jim. He grabbed her around the waist and pushed her aside.

"What is it?" he said sharply.

Gail was shaking. "I'm not sure. I. . .I think a snake just . . .just. . . ."

"It didn't bite you, did it?"

"No, no. I nearly trod on something as it went across the path."

Jim quickly moved to turn on the laundry light again, much to Bonnie's delight, and peered out across the uncut lawn.

"I can't see anything, now. You run onto the patio while I leave this light on."

Gail fled. Jim joined her a moment later. Her face was still very pale and her lips were trembling as she faced him.

"I hate snakes!" she said passionately.

"Don't we all! Oh, Gail, you poor dear."

As though of their own volition, Jim's arms reached out and pulled her into that comforting haven she had known before. Her body was still trembling and he held her closer as though to stop it with his own strength. It suddenly had the opposite effect—her trembling increased.

Gail felt Jim's body tremble in response. She lifted her head and her eyes searched his. Unmistakable passion filled his with a brilliance she could hardly believe. Then his head descended and she gasped as his lips captured hers.

The kiss was timeless. Warmth flooded through Gail's body and she felt as though her whole being was quickening with new life—with love.

Then, suddenly, the spell was broken. Jim wrenched himself away. Gail swayed at the sudden loss of support. She murmured an automatic protest and would have moved towards him.

His agonized, convulsed face stopped her. He opened his mouth to speak as a chill crept over her. He clamped his lips shut, and she saw him close his eyes tightly and swallow before trying again. She stood frozen and watched him with a dawning anguish of her own.

"I'm most terribly sorry, Gail. I...I had no right to kiss you like that. Would you please forgive me? It won't happen again."

The words seemed torn from him. And then the screen door banged and he was gone.

eight

The harvest commenced the next day in sweltering heat. After a sleepless night, Gail forced herself out of bed when the alarm rang. Her first desire after going to her room had been to pack her bags. The confirmation of Hilda's claim hurt unbearably. But, there was the harvest. There was Marian and the children. Heavy-eyed, she made her way to the kitchen to find Mrs. Stevens already in control.

"Good morning, Gail. I believe you had trouble with Bonnie last night?"

"Did...did Jim get up to go to her again? I'm afraid I just stayed in bed and listened to her yelping."

She avoided the sharp look Marian flashed at her while she continued making the children's lunches. "You...and Jim, too, for that matter, certainly look as though you didn't get much sleep last night."

Gail felt a wave of warmth creep into her cheeks. She busied herself pouring out a cup of tea before answering in a deliberately casual voice. "I did get some sleep." She didn't add that it wasn't until dawn before she had been able to drift into an unrefreshing doze. "Has Jim slept in?" she said instead.

"Oh, no. He's been up for ages. We won't see him now until smoke-o time."

"Smoke-o?"

Marian grinned. "Not heard that one? Morning tea to

you. The header will be rolling as soon as the moisture content allows."

"Oh, yes, I think I remember Will telling me once that with bulk handling it was no good starting until the dew had dried off the grain. Phew! It's so hot I shouldn't think it will take long today."

"Yes, that's right," Marian said a little absent-mindedly. "Gail, once you get back from taking the children up to get the bus, we'll have to start packing the smoke-o things. I'll go out with you today, but in the future it will be your job to take it out to the men. I'm afraid my silly old asthma doesn't like all the dust stirred up. Now, I think it's time the children were up."

There was apparently going to be no time for leisurely cups of tea with breakfast while the harvest was on, Gail realized as she quickly swallowed the remainder of hers and raced off to see to the children.

That day set the pattern for the next couple of weeks. In blistering heat, the paddocks were reaped one by one. Jim had employed a couple of truck drivers and someone to relieve him on the header at times. Jim and Gail managed to avoid each other as much as possible and only exchanged such stilted conversation that Gail noticed Marian frown in bewilderment at them a few times, although in some strange way she also seemed relieved.

Except when the whole family went to church each Sunday, Marian never left the house during those hectic days. Gail ferried the thermos flasks of tea as well as cool drinks with boxes of food to and fro over the denuded paddocks. She learned to carefully drive the Holden in the tracks made by the trucks and utility as she made her way across the stubble to where the header was eating deeper and deeper into the golden wheat.

She had little time to think during the day. At night, she was too exhausted to lie awake for long brooding on her growing love for Jim. For, try as she might, day by day she found her feelings deepening. The memory of that kiss could not be banished. No matter that she called herself a fool innumerable times. No matter that after his distressed apology there had been no need to ask about Hilda. Although there had been no occasion for them to be alone since that night, sometimes Gail had caught him looking at her. But, he had avoided her eyes, and now she was more and more sure the agony she had seen in his face had been because of his shame at having yielded to a momentary temptation.

Gail suspected that Jim's devotion to Christ would have made him feel his failure toward Hilda very deeply. She knew that even on the most demanding day he still managed to have his devotional times. Once, she had gone to put away some of his washed and ironed clothes after tea when she had thought he was still watching the news on television. Without knocking, she had pushed open the door of his room only to retreat very quickly as she caught a glimpse of the dark figure on his knees beside his bed. That had disturbed her as nothing else did during that time.

Table devotions each night were continued even when Jim was unable to share the evening meal with them.

"Gail, would you mind reading the Bible for us tonight?" Marion had asked one evening.

Gail had glanced at her drawn, pale face and readily agreed. After that, she found herself actually offering to read. She had been ashamed of how awkward and shy she had felt that first time but, without her even being aware of it, she had grown to enjoy those times. At first, she had tried to tell herself it was because it was all part of feeling a member of a family again. Then, she knew that the Word she had heard and had read herself was beginning to challenge her.

Once, she had not understood a passage, and had finally plucked up the courage to ask Marian what it meant. She had been answered so matter of factly and without the least hint of preaching at her, that she had been encouraged from then on to continue asking at various times about things she had heard at church as well as from the readings.

Little did she know how the older woman quietly rejoiced at Gail's increasing interest in spiritual things.

Gail had eventually written to Sister Drew.

"I haven't mentioned that silly name change business, yet," she had written briefly. "There just hasn't seemed to be an appropriate time, although I was able to tell Jim about the accident. It doesn't really matter anymore, but if it worries you, I promise to tell them after the harvest."

She did not add that she shrank from forcing a private conversation with Jim because of the tension between them. She knew that after the harvest she would have to leave anyway. There was no way she could bear to be there when Hilda and Jim announced their engagement.

And then, one day, more letters from Ann Green and Sister Drew arrived.

The day had started badly. Gail had forgotten to wind her alarm clock. Marian had banged on her door, and then put her head around the corner and grinned as Gail raised a dazed face.

"You're late, sleepyhead. You've only half an hour to get up and leave for the school bus."

It was a mad scramble, but they just made it, Gail pulling up the car with a crunch of gravel and slight squeal of brakes as she saw the bus waiting.

"Phew! Nice going, Gail," said Will as he hopped out of the car. "You'll make a rally car driver after all," he yelled over his shoulder as he took off after the children.

Gail waited to wave the bus off before starting back. To her utter dismay, about two kilometers from the farm, the engine suddenly cut out. Gail managed to steer the car onto the grass before the vehicle stopped rolling.

She turned the ignition and tried to start the motor. Then she remembered, and glanced at the petrol gauge. Yesterday morning Jim had warned her to take the car down to the sheds and fill the petrol tank from the farm's barrel.

"Rally driver! Like fun!' she fumed as she began the long, hot walk across the paddocks to the house.

Fortunately, Jim was at the sheds, and she was grateful for his restraint when he quickly filled a can of petrol and drove her back to the car.

When he had finished pouring the petrol into the car, he straightened wearily and turned toward her. Suddenly, she felt breathless, and couldn't look away from that blue gaze. A grease-stained hand left a smear on his cheek as he wiped his hand over his face.

"Look, Gail, we've got to talk," he suddenly said urgently, "not now, but soon."

They stared at each other silently. Then she nodded abruptly and managed a brief smile before driving away.

For the rest of the morning, she thought about what they might say to each other.

It had been a bad start to a day that gradually went from bad to worse.

After returning from delivering a hastily prepared, but still late smoke-o to the disgruntled header driver, Gail noticed that Marian was pale and she insisted that she lie down for a while. She flew at the preparations for lunch, determined that there would be no more cause for complaints, but had just finished making the tea when she heard a vehicle stop outside.

"Anyone home?"

"Oh, no!" she muttered to herself as she recognized Hilda's voice. "In the kitchen," she called out.

"Oh, it's you." Hilda's lilting tones went flat as she saw Gail. She peered around the kitchen.

"Mrs. Stevens out?"

"No, she's resting."

"Oh, the poor dear! She must be exhausted! I'll go and see what I can do for her."

Before Gail could remonstrate, she had disappeared down the hall in the direction of the bedrooms. She hesitated for a moment and then shrugged. If anyone could handle Hilda, her future mother-in-law could.

The thought stabbed at her and unexpected tears sprang to her eyes. She brushed them away angrily. Silly fool. Only, how she would have loved having Marian for her own mother-in-law!

The screen door banged. It was the truck driver with a message from Jim. She had to race into Toowoomba for a spare part for a broken down header.

Gail was away for most of the afternoon. It was a quick trip in and straight back to where Jim was working on the header, but it was nearly three hours later before Gail found herself back in the kitchen.

Apparently, Hilda had long gone home. Marian took one look at Gail's exhausted face as she entered the kitchen and made her sit down straight away.

"I'll make you a cup of coffee, love, while you sit there for a few minutes. I'm afraid it's nearly time for you to meet the school bus, too. But the kids can wait a couple of minutes while you recover."

"Is it always as hectic as this at harvest time?" Gail asked in a tired voice, and then added, "I think I'd better make myself a sandwich, too."

"Gail! You did have some lunch, didn't you?"

She was horrified when Gail confessed there had not been time before, and insisted on Gail finishing every crumb of the food she placed in front of her.

"It won't be the first or the last time the children have had to walk part of the way home," she said. "I wish Jim would let me drive, but I'm afraid that rotten arthritis is making itself felt today." She smiled at Gail's murmur of sympathy. "It's just one of those things I can expect to get gradually worse. On your way back, don't forget the mail, will you. I'm hoping for a letter from Beth today."

Mrs. Stevens had at last told Jim about Beth's request for him to go down to Sydney again. They had both agreed that another trip was impossible until after the harvest unless there was a marked change in Arthur's condition. There had been a brief phone call from Beth after that, assuring them that the doctors said there had been no actual worsening of the paralysis but his whole attitude toward the possibility of being a permanent invalid was causing increasing concern.

Gail picked up the three children almost halfway home from the bus stop. Will was very quiet, but the children were decidedly grumpy from the heat and their tired feet. She stopped and picked up the mailbag, but they were all too busy with the evening chores to be able to open it.

The three youngsters were roped in to assist with the clearing away of the meal. Jim's tea was put aside to be heated up in the microwave, so Marian went to the lounge room with the mailbag. When Gail at last joined her, she raised a strained face from reading a letter.

"There's a couple for you, Gail," she said abruptly, and buried her head again in her letter.

Gail hesitated, hoping nothing had happened in Sydney; then she glanced at her own mail, knowing she would see Sister Drew's handwriting.

"I'm so tired I think I'll see that the children are okay and then go straight to bed," she said slowly. "Have you any idea how long Jim will be?"

"What's that, Gail?" Marian raised her head and looked blankly at Gail for a moment. "Oh, Jim shouldn't be much longer. He has to finish welding in the shed. The rest will have to be done as soon as it's light enough in the paddock." She gave herself a slight shake, and looked at Gail intently. "Look, why don't you go to bed right away. I can keep an eye on the children and fix Jim up. You look exhausted."

Gail ran her hand through her hair. "If you're sure you

aren't too tired, also, I'll do just that. In fact, I think I'll race everyone else to the bath now."

Gail waited until she was lying on her bed before opening her letters. She opened the one from Ann first. Gail had answered her last one briefly by saying that she was helping out some old friends of Sister Drew's, and would contact her again when she eventually went back to Sydney.

This letter from Ann went to the point very quickly. A friend of Ann's was nursing the truck driver who had been left paralyzed. The doctors and nursing staff were becoming increasingly concerned about his mental state. Apparently, he had begun to refuse some of the treatments just when there had been several indications that the paralysis may not be as permanent or as extensive as originally thought.

Ann's friend had managed to get closer to him on night duty than the rest of the staff. From several things he had let slip in the quiet hours of the night, she was convinced that Gail held the key to his depression.

So far they had been fairly successful in keeping from his wife how alarmed the staff was becoming about him. It couldn't be long before she would have to be told.

Ann's closing comments were blunt. "Rightly or wrongly, Gail, you blame Art Smith for the death of your folk. When the court case comes up he may be punished or cleared of negligence. If you do not go and see this man, you yourself may very well be guilty of depriving that woman and her two children of an active husband and father. In fact, Liz was warned to be extra careful with any drugs in his room and to be watchful in case he tries to harm himself. Could you ever forgive yourself if he committed suicide?"

Gail read and reread that last sentence. She had not known the man had a wife and two children. Her hand clenched on the letter with dawning horror.

Beth had two children. Beth's husband was paralyzed. Beth was worried because the accident was preying on his mind.

Gail closed her eyes and saw Marian looking the way she did the day of the picnic when she had lifted her head and looked steadily at Gail. Jim had interrupted them and Gail had been so aware of him that she had not taken in what his mother had been saying.

It couldn't be. It must not be. She had to know for sure.

In a daze, Gail stood up and walked from the bedroom. The lounge was empty. She hesitated, undecided whether to follow Marian to her room.

No. Jim. She had to find Jim.

Jim had only sketchily washed his face and hands before getting his tea, and was sitting wearily at the kitchen table eating his late meal. He looked up with bloodshot, dust-filled eyes at Gail as she stood in the doorway.

"Sorry about the filthy clothes, Gail. I was starving and—"

"Jim."

He stared at her curiously as she interrupted him, and waited.

"Jim," she said again, and this time something in her voice and face reached him through the haze of exhaustion. "Jim, what's Beth's husband's name?" Gail put her trembling hand to her mouth and waited.

"Beth?" replied Jim in a puzzled voice. "She's just plain

Smith. I believe Arthur's name used to be Canley-Smith at one stage, but he's always just called himself Smith."

She was like a statue. Her lips felt stiff. Then, as she saw the growing concern in his face, she forced herself to say, "Isn't that strange. All the weeks I've been here, I've never once heard. . .heard the children's surname. . .or Beth's. I didn't know her name. I just did not know, Jim. Will. . .will you remember that? I just didn't. . . ."

She turned and walked slowly back to her room on shaking legs. She stood beside her bed with the letter still crushed in her hand. Sister Drew's letter was still waiting to be read. She opened it slowly, knowing what she would read.

It held a direct request from the doctor in charge of Art Smith to go and visit him as soon as possible. Written about the same time as Ann's, the letter contained the information that, after numerous infections, he was building up the resistance to antibiotics that paraplegics sometimes did. His last infection had taken a long time to control and they were fearful for him if he should have another. He was in a very depressed state and the nursing staff was finding it increasingly difficult to make him take any medication and treatment.

Gail was a little puzzled that Sister Drew seemed to take for granted that Gail already knew she was living with Arthur's family. The general tone of the letter was abrupt. Sister Drew did not know how Gail could continue with her bitter attitude towards Arthur when she professed to be so fond of his in-laws and, above all, his delightful children. The letter ended abruptly. If she would let her know when she was arriving, she would meet her at the airport. She was only "yours faithfully" at the conclusion of the letter.

As Gail stared blindly at the letter, she heard a gentle rap on her door.

"Are you all right, Gail?" Jim called softly.

It took her a moment to find her voice.

"I'll be fine, Jim."

There was a brief pause and then he called, "Good night then," before she heard his steps moving away.

Gail knew she had no choice. She had to leave as soon as possible. Her suitcases were stacked on top of the large wardrobe. Jumping to her feet, she feverishly grabbed a chair and climbed up on to it so she could reach them. The chair tilted and she almost lost her balance as she lifted them down. Her heart pounded with shock and fright at the thought of hurting herself and not being able to leave the next day.

She collapsed on the bed, gulping in deep breaths. The suitcases were sprawled across the floor. She looked at them and felt the wetness of tears and realized for the first time that she was crying. What was she going to do? Where would she end up? She was homeless again.

The words of the hymn flashed into her mind, "Take it to the Lord in prayer." Without afterwards knowing quite how she got there, she found herself on her knees, beside her bed, for the very first time. She couldn't even remember afterwards if she had actually articulated any words. Her whole being just seemed to reach out to God.

Gradually, her tears stopped; a long time later, she stood up. Her mind was functioning again now. She thought about Arthur Smith. The fact remained that he was still responsible for her family's death.

She looked across at the photographs. If it had not been for him, they would still be here. But, even if she did go to see him, could she assure him that she had really forgiven him?

She suddenly realized that he was not only responsible for the death of her family, but he was also the reason she had to leave this place of refuge. But then, if he were not in the hospital, she would probably have never met Jim.

And never learned to love him, she thought bitterly.

Her mouth set firmly. One thing was sure—she had to return to Sydney at once. She could not stay here another day. The Garretts had already finished their smaller acreage of wheat to be harvested. If help was needed, Marian would have to put up with Hilda for the last few days of harvest.

She began to pack the cases.

nine

Gail managed only a couple of hours of deep, exhausted sleep. As she at last stumbled out of bed, she refused to allow herself to think. The morning was considerably cooler and so she dressed quickly in the slack suit she had worn to the farm. It brought back memories of Jim's gentleness when she had been sick beside the car.

Without realizing it, she slipped into the pattern so recently conquered of forcing her mind not to dwell on hurtful memories. So, she began planning all that had to be done before she could leave. She knew there were several flights out of Brisbane for Sydney every day. The main thing was to leave as soon as possible. Someone would have to take her to Toowoomba at least, and then there would be buses or. . . .

While she was decisively stripping her bed, she heard the phone ringing. She glanced at her watch. It was still very early. Who could be ringing at this early hour?

The phone was located a little way up the corridor from Gail's bedroom. When she left her room, she saw with surprise that it was Jim who had answered it. What even surprised her more was that he was still in his pajamas and bathrobe. Usually, by this time, he had long since gone down to the sheds to check everything for the day's work.

As she saw him, he put down the receiver and turned toward her. His face was alight with happiness that dimmed a little as his gaze swept over Gail.

Moving towards her he said, "That was Beth and—who told you this is the day to get on our good duds to go to town?"

Gail blinked. "This is the day we go to town?"

He began to laugh at her, and then stopped and looked a little puzzled.

"Isn't that why you're all dressed up? When it rains, we usually grab the chance to race into town."

"When it rains?" asked Gail stupidly.

"Didn't you hear it teeming down in the early hours? Boy, you must have been sleeping the sleep of the just! Lady, it really rained last night!"

Gail winced. She saw a swift frown momentarily crease his forehead. "Does that mean the harvest can't be finished?" she rushed to say, "And doesn't that mean you'll lose a lot of money?"

She was relieved to see the twinkle of amusement sweep back into his eyes. "You city slicker! If it keeps raining, the harvest may very well be finished, and, yes, we would lose a lot of money. But the sun is shining this morning. It just means that for today we don't work." He looked rueful. "I was thinking of all that hard work yesterday to get the header working again. It could have been done today."

Gail was watching him intently as he talked. It passed through her mind that this might be the last time he talked so freely to her. He would soon know. She caught her breath sharply. Perhaps now was the time. But suddenly she couldn't bear the thought of his knowing how bitter and unforgiving she had been.

Jim had been studying the changing expressions on her

face as he talked, and must have seen the bleak look flash into her eyes.

"You are really taking this harvest to heart, aren't you, Gail." His eyes were tender. "That storm just means the black soil will be too sticky for at least today for the trucks and header. The grain will have to dry out, too, before we start again."

He paused, and impulsively grabbed her hand. She snatched it away as though he had scorched her. The bright expression on his face disappeared.

"Anyway, we have to make a trip to Brisbane today as it happens," he said briskly. "Beth's coming home."

Gail froze. Her mouth went dry and she couldn't think of one word to say. Was this just a coincidence? She suddenly remembered what Marian had said once about coincidences.

"So many things happen in a person's life that appear to be coincidences. But some people can see God's help and direction in them and in those apparently 'lucky breaks.' "

And she had pleaded for God's help last night.

Gail mentally shook herself. It must be just that Beth wanted to see the children. Jim was directing one of his soul searching looks at her.

"That was a phone call from Beth," he began slowly, "Arthur has insisted she come home for a few days and so she's decided she can't last another minute without seeing her two offspring again. She's catching the midday plane. Gail, is anything—"

"Jim! Who was on the phone so early. Is everything all right? It wasn't Beth, was it?"

Jim swung around to his mother and began telling her about Beth.

Gail closed her eyes. It didn't make sense. Why was Arthur sending his wife home? Those letters from Ann and Sister Drew had taken a few days to reach her. Was the hospital staff right to be worried about his depression? Or was he starting to improve? Beth would never have left him unless he had persuaded her. . .convinced her. . . .

Something was wrong. A sense of fear and urgency began to surge through Gail. She had to get to Sydney before tonight.

Jim had been explaining to his mother and Gail heard her delighted exclamation. They came towards Gail and Marian stopped and looked with a puzzled frown at Gail's clothes.

"What are you dressed up for, Gail? I didn't know you were planning on going anywhere."

Gail looked at her speechlessly. She didn't know where to begin or what to say.

Marian Stevens stared back. She suddenly stiffened. Gail saw an eager, excited expression fill her face.

Gail's legs felt weak. She knew. Somehow, Marian knew.

"Gail?" All the pleading and hope she couldn't put into words were in the slightly husky voice.

"Yes," said Gail simply.

"Hey, you two! What's going on?"

Jim had caught the inflecton in his mother's voice and was looking from one to another with a worried expression.

Marian kept looking steadily at Gail. She answered him

very slowly, relief beginning to glow in her face.

"I believe Gail has decided she has to go back to Sydney today. Is that right, Gail?"

"Yes," was all Gail could still find to say.

"Back to Sydney! Today? Are you both crazy or something? Beth's coming today and you're leaving? What on earth's going on?" Jim's face was a picture of bewilderment and dawning anger.

Gail looked at him, and found her voice at last. "I've just got to go today," she managed to say quietly and firmly. She hesitated and her eyes locked with Marian's again. "And apparently your mother knows why," she finished appealingly.

"Well, why then?" Jim snapped. He ran his hand over his face and Gail began to tremble.

"Oh, please. Please, Jim. I don't think I can tell you. I'd rather you didn't know until I'm gone. Please, Marian. . . ."

"It's all right, Gail." She moved forward quickly and placed her hand on Gail's arm.

"It's not all right!" Jim began furiously. "I demand an explanation. What could be important enough to make you leave us in the lurch in the middle of harvest? And when will you be back? You do intend to come back?"

The increasing anguish on Gail's face brought him to an abrupt halt. He looked helplessly at his mother, some of that anguish dawning in his own eyes.

"Mum? We can't lose Gail. Not now. Not yet." His voice was quieter, pleading now.

His mother looked at him gently. She attempted a smile. "God knows best, son," she reminded him. Unquenchable faith shone in her face.

He stared at her dumbly. She looked back at him with compassion.

Gail glanced from one to the other. They were communicating without words. There was pain in Jim's face. Her heart leaped. For her?

Jim closed his eyes. He rocked gently on his feet for a moment. Gail saw his lips move. For one incredible moment, she thought he was praying as she had seen people silently do so at the little church as they had been handed communion.

Then he opened his eyes and looked at Gail. Her hopes died as she saw him square his shoulders. The anger was completely gone from his face.

"We'll just have to leave it to Him to sort out then, won't we?" he said steadily, and then turned and strode down the hallway to his room.

I don't know how God could work any of this mess out, Gail thought off and on during the next hectic hour or so. A phone call had secured a seat on a plane for her and then it had been decided, to Gail's relief, that the two excited children would accompany her and Jim to Brisbane. Marian decided not to go. She said it would be better if she did some of the necessary preparation and work for when the harvest resumed.

Gail looked at her doubtfully. There had been no return of any chest problems and she seemed very well, but Gail knew how tired she still was some evenings. She suspected there would be a marathon of baking as soon as they were gone. However, there was nothing she could do except work as hard as she could in the few minutes left and try to leave as little as possible of the housework undone.

The children were more excited and thrilled than Gail had ever seen them. She had not realized how much they had missed their mother. They had spoken to her on the phone quite often and, as Gail thought over the past weeks, she wondered how she could have been so blind as not to realize before that Beth's husband and the children's father was the same man that Sister had been so concerned about.

For the first time Gail found herself thinking of Art—or Arthur—Smith as a person in his own right, and not some drunken monster who had been responsible for all her misery. She wondered about him now. What had he and Beth quarreled about so bitterly that he had walked out? Now he was an invalid. Would this be a permanent reconciliation?

The brief time left on the farm flew by. The children's joy at seeing their mother again had been blunted when they found out that Gail was leaving. For a moment, Robbie's bottom lip quivered. Marian quickly reminded him that they had Bonnie to introduce to his mother. At that he brightened up and dragged Jacky out to make sure Bonnie's coat was brushed until it shone. After that, there was plenty to do to keep them—and Gail—busy until it was time to go.

At last, Jim—a quiet, stern Jim—began to pack Gail's things in the car. Gail was in her bedroom when he returned for the last case. They stood and looked at each other for a long moment. She longed to tell him that Hilda was not good enough for him and that she, Gail, needed his strength and his love. Once, she thought he was going to speak. But then he set his lips grimly and turned away without a word.

Gail crossed the room and stared out of the window across the forlorn looking paddocks. All the wheat within her view had been reaped. She had often wondered what it was like here when the frost was on the ground. Stories had been told to her of the frozen pipes that had burst, of the radiators on vehicles that had to be protected.

She wanted to see those grim paddocks softened by the gentle green of the newly shooting wheat. She wanted to be able to see the seasons come and go. Jim had told he was planning to plant sorghum for the next crop. She had told him she wasn't sure if she knew what that looked liked. He had laughed at her a little and told her that she still had a lot to learn.

Now, she yearned to live all her tomorrows here with Jim.

The sun's rays were glinting on a few puddles of rain water. It seemed impossible that she had slept so soundly that the drumming of the rain on the roof had not awakened her. *If only tomorrow would come like that,* she thought. *A deep, peaceful sleep while the storm blew itself out. Then, when you woke, the sun would be shining again.*

They were all outside near the Holden when Gail let the screen door bang for the last time.

"Come on, Gail," called Will impatiently. He was being dropped off at the school bus stop on the way.

There had been no chance for Gail and Marian to speak privately. She went over to Gail, standing on the path beneath the trees.

Once, it would have been natural for Gail to lean over and kiss the lined cheek goodbye. Now, Gail stood looking at her uncertainly. Jim glanced at them briefly and made a business of settling the others in the car.

Gail blinked the ready tears away as she realized there was little likelihood she would see this fine woman ever again.

"I hope you don't hate me too much," she whispered.

Marian's eyes widened in astonishment. "Hate you?" she exclaimed in distress. "Have I given you the impression these last few weeks that I have hated you?"

It was Gail's turn to be surprised. "You mean you've known all that time? I thought your mail last night—"

"No, No! Jean phoned me that first Sunday, while you were still asleep. You looked so pale and strained that evening that I couldn't say anything. Then, when I thought about it, I wanted you to get to know us better. I kept hoping you would feel free to tell us of your own accord. That day of the picnic...I...I was about to say something when Jim interrupted us. I had faith in your own basic character, my dear. We are kindred spirits in so many ways. I really enjoyed being your...your mother for a little while. All this time you've been recovering from the shock of it all. I've prayed that healing would come and...well, I knew God would work it all out in His good time."

A warm glow had begun to spread though Gail's body. Until then she had not realized how cold and numbed she had been throughout the hectic rush of the morning.

"You knew," she murmured, "all this time you've known. You've put your arms around me and...and...."

Those warm, loving arms were holding her close again.

Gail did not see Jim looking across at them. He was looking at his mother with love and pride. He had been too far away to hear their conversation. He took a step as though to go to the two women. Then his hands clenched. He paused, and opened the car door instead. He climbed in and slammed it shut with unnecessary force.

The sound made Marian let Gail go. They both had to brush the tears away. Each gave the other rather watery smiles as they did so. The frozen look was gone from Gail's dark brown eyes.

"Jim's getting impatient. You must go. But Gail, my dear, we won't lose touch."

Gail found there were no words to express how she was feeling and turned and went across to the car. She dared not look at Jim as they moved slowly down the rough driveway made even worse by the heavy trucks. She waved goodbye to Marian Stevens until she was out of sight, knowing also she was saying goodbye to the house and farm that had become home for such a brief time. She choked back the tears that threatened. Merely keeping in touch but no longer being such as intimate part of all of this would be unbearable. She would, no doubt, write to them a few times. But she would never be back because of Jim, and especially not because of Hilda.

There was very little conversation between Jim and Gail on the trip to Brisbane. When they were driving past the beautiful Queen's Park in Toowoomba, Gail felt sad because there had been no time to really explore this lovely city perched on the top of the mountain range.

"We never did get a chance to bring you to Toowoomba

for the day. I wanted to show you the view from Picnic Point—" Jim stopped abruptly, as though regretting his words.

Gail murmured something in response and, for a moment, their glances met. Her own sadness was reflected in his eyes. After that, she avoided looking at him and was bitterly aware that he never glanced at her once. She knew that Jim would be too courteous to show her how annoyed and dismayed he was with her for letting him down. But Beth might be able to stay and help until after the harvest. And there was always Hilda.

There was much she longed to say to him, but she was silent, and let the children's chatter go unchecked. They stopped only once for a refreshment break, and were just on time at the airport.

However, to Gail's dismay, her flight was delayed. It had been scheduled to take off a few minutes before Beth was due to arrive. She did not want to meet Beth. She had not asked Marian if Beth knew who she was, but she probably did by now. Perhaps that was even her main reason for coming home.

Beth's plane arrived a few minutes later.

Gail watched Robbie and Jacky race over to the slight, unexpectedly fair-haired woman who knelt down to hug and kiss them. Beth stood up and kissed Jim. The tears were still glistening on her cheeks when she turned to Gail. They stared at each other. Although she was fair where Jim was dark, her eyes were as blue as his.

To Gail's absolute horror, she saw all the warmth start to drain from them as Jim's sister stared at her.

The loudspeaker sprang into life, announcing

Gail's flight.

"Oh, Gail. What a shame. You've got to go," said Jim quickly. "Beth, I'm afraid you'll have to say a very quick hello and goodbye to the friend of Aunt Jean who has been helping us out."

Beth's smile had completely disappeared while Jim was talking. Her lips tightened. Gail saw recognition and bitterness fill her face.

"You! So you were here all the time. I suppose you've been gloating all this time over Arthur's punishment."

"Beth!" Jim was looking at his sister in disbelief and horror. "What on earth's the matter with you? This is Gail who—"

"I know who she is! Abigail Brandon! I've studied her photo often enough, wondering how anyone so beautiful on the outside could be so hard and unforgiving on the inside. You should be thanking God you are alive, or not still in hospital, like my husband."

Gail dared to glance quickly at Jim. His face was a mixture of bewilderment and dawning comprehension. He put his hand on Beth's arm and tried to stop the flow of brutal words. She shook him off and turned on him. Her face was pale and anguished. Her eyes shot sparks of fire.

"How could you, Jim!" she spat at him. "How could you have her looking after my children. Abigail Brandon! The girl who refuses to—"

Gail heard with relief the final urgent call to board the plane. She knew she couldn't take anymore. She felt sick and shaken. Her eyes locked with Jim's as she desperately interrupted the angry words.

"I've got to go, Jim. To. . .to see Arthur. And. . .

and. . . ." Tears blurred her last sight of him. "Please, don't judge me too harshly. Your mother, she'll tell you. . .tell you. . . ."

Gail turned and ran towards the gate where the hostesses were already on their way to the plane. She thought she heard Jim's voice shouting after her, but she kept running.

Vaguely, she knew people were turning and watching her curiously. All Gail had mirrored on her mind was the horror in Jim's eyes.

ten

The hour that passed before the Boeing jet touched down at Mascot always remained a blur of pain in Gail's memory.

She spent most of the flight hunched miserably in her seat. Vaguely, she realized that the passenger next to her and the hostesses were concerned about her. She looked at them with dazed eyes and numbly shook her head at their offers of cups of tea and magazines, until they left her alone.

How Jim must be despising her! To have her time with that delightful family end like this was devastating.

And the children! They had been clinging to their mother's hands. Their eyes had grown huge with fear and dismay at the angry words directed at their beloved Gail. Their much awaited reunion was thoroughly spoiled.

Beth. Never before had anyone stared at Gail with such bitterness and hatred.

And she was Jim's sister.

The gentle jolt as the wheels touched on the Tarmac and the increased roar of the jets brought Gail back to an awareness of her surroundings. She turned her head and caught the concerned look of the elderly man sitting beside her.

"Ah. That's better, my dear," he said softly.

Gail stared at him blankly, and then a tinge of color

swept into her ashen cheeks as she realized the spectacle she must have made of herself.

"It's all right. You don't have to be embarrassed." The stranger's voice was gentle and sympathetic. "We all have times of pain and anguish in this old world."

The plane began to taxi along the runway to the terminal buildings. The hostesses began moving up and down the aisles again. One of them paused and glanced keenly at Gail. She gave her a relieved smile before hurrying on.

"We've been concerned about you," the gentle voice beside her went on.

Gail's throat was dry and sore. No tears had fallen, but her eyes were burning. "I'm sorry," she began in a hoarse whisper.

"No, no, my dear. You don't have to apologise." The man paused.

Gail turned and looked at him again. He was very old, and watching her with a considering look.

"I've been hoping though that I might have an opportunity of saying something to you." He hesitated again. The plane was drawing to a stop. The man continued speaking with an urgency that caught Gail's attention. "My dear, I'm an old man now and have known much sorrow. I just want to tell you that God longs to be your friend and comfort and strength in times of pain and despair. He has been my constant companion and friend for well over sixty years and has never let me down. He loves you and longs for you to turn to Him. He—"

"Come on, Dad. Time to go."

Gail watched dumbly as the smiling, gray-haired lady released the old man's seat belt and helped him to his feet.

He resisted the pull on his arm for a moment and looked back at Gail. Love and longing reached out to her. "Oh, I do pray that you will reach out to Him. He'll be there—always!"

For a few moments, Gail sat very still as the passengers moved slowly down the aisle. At last, she stirred and joined the stream of people.

There was some delay with the unloading of the plane. Gail made her way to a coffee lounge, suddenly realizing how little she had managed to swallow all day. Mechanically, she ordered some sandwiches and coffee that she forced herself to eat. As she began to feel a little better, she realized it was the same place she had been in before going on the trip north. Only a few weeks had passed since she had waited here, wondering and worrying if she were doing the right thing.

Gail suddenly remembered how Jim's warm smile, just before he left her to find his own seat on the plane, had somehow given her hope that perhaps she had found a new life and reason for living. And she had found a new life. The love and acceptance she had found had brought healing to her wounded heart and mind. But now new sorrow had replaced the old.

"He loves you and longs for you to turn to Him."

Somebody else besides the old man had said those same words. Gail thought back over the few past weeks. Then, she remembered. It had been the Reverend Telford who had said those words. He had at first seemed such a quiet, unassuming young man when she had met him just before the service, but his sermon had been unexpectedly full of vim and passion. He had gazed longingly over the congregation and said those very same words the old man had just repeated. "He loves you, and longs for you to turn to Him."

She had been waiting for an opportunity to ask Jim or his mother about some of the other things he had also mentioned. And now she never would.

Gail's hand shook. She hastily put down the cup of hot coffee. Jim had said he was preaching again this coming Sunday, and she had been longing forward to it. Now. . . .

Perhaps Sister Drew would know some answers to the questions that were burning inside her.

Sister Drew.

Gail straightened. She had forgotten to ring her and let her know she was coming. And Art Smith. She still had to make sure he was not planning something very foolish.

The taxi driver couldn't have been more helpful and even carried her cases up the steps of the Nurses' Home and into the front entrance before giving her a cheerful wave goodbye. Gail left the luggage piled in the corridor and went straight to the Nurse Educator's office. She took a deep breath before raising her hand and knocking on the door.

She felt like a different person than the one who had been about to knock on this door only a few weeks ago. She could think about the accident without that sick churning inside her. Other people now occupied her attention; before she continually thought only of her own circumstances. Only one thing seemed to be the same. Her lips tilted wryly. She was still just a little scared of Sister Drew.

The familiar voice called out to her to come in, and she opened the door.

Sister Drew's head was bowed over her desk as her pen flew over some papers. "Be with you in a minute, Nurse. I've nearly finished this report for you."

Gail hesitated, then said softly, "Good afternoon, Sister."

Sister Drew's head jerked up. "Gail!"

She jumped to her feet and hurried around the desk. Gail breathed a faint sigh of relief at the beaming smile that lit the alert face. Two hands gripped Gail's shoulders and she unbelievingly felt a kiss on her cheek. This was a welcome she hadn't dreamed of.

"Oh, my dear girl, I'm so glad you've come!"

It was too much. The tears started pouring down Gail's face.

Sister gave a startled exclamation and put Gail gently into a chair. The floodgates were open and she only vaguely heard the knock on the door and Sister Drew speaking softly to someone.

She tried to pull herself together and had partly succeeded when she felt a comforting hand stroking her bowed head.

"You poor girl. Has it been that bad?" A box of tissues was offered, and the sympathetic voice continued. "Jim rang me a little while ago. He was worried about you."

"Jim rang!"

"Yes. From the Brisbane airport. He told me what had happened."

Gail swallowed on more tears. "Beth, she. . .she hates me. She thinks I went up there on purpose. To gloat. She—"

"Oh no, no. Of course she doesn't. Not now anyway. I

told Jim it was all my idea. That you didn't have the faintest idea. He had already told Beth that anyway before he rang."

"He'd told Beth that?"

"Yes. Apparently you asked him last night what Beth's name was and he guessed the rest."

"Oh. Yes, so I did."

Sister Drew perched on the edge of the desk; she looked puzzled. "But I don't understand. You must have known before last night that they were Arthur's folk. When I wrote to you that first week I thought I said something about it then."

"I've been so dumb. You only said that by then I'd know what the rest of your plan had been. I. . .I thought you meant something else. And somehow I just never even heard what Robbie and Jacky's surname was.

There was a knock on the door and a nurse entered carrying an afternoon tea tray. She looked curiously at Gail.

"Thank you, Nurse. And now you can deliver this report to Miss Fisher for me. And don't dawdle, girl!"

The old familiar battle-ax bite had crept into the Sister's voice. Gail grinned weakly as twinkling eyes were turned on her after the flustered nurse had shot out of the room.

"Got to keep them up to the mark," Sister Drew said cheerfully. She poured out the tea and waited until Gail had managed a few sips and felt her trembling gradually ease.

"And what do you want to do now, Gail," she asked with a hint of anxiety.

"I'm not sure." Gail rubbed her eyes again. "I think I've been in a daze ever since reading those letters last night."

"Letters?"

"Yes. Ann Green wrote to me, too. Her friend is one of the night nurses looking after Art—Arthur Smith." Gail hesitated, and then said slowly, "I think it's really her letter as much as anything that made me know I had to come as soon as possible. Do you know if the doctors think he is so depressed he could. . .would try and deliberately harm himself? And I don't understand why Beth went home when she did. Is there a marked improvement in him by any chance?"

Sister Drew looked startled. "I haven't heard any suggestion about that, Gail." She thought for a moment. "Perhaps because they know I'm a personal friend of the family they may have been afraid to say anything in case I mentioned it to Beth." There was a snort. "As though any nurse worth her salt would discuss something like that with a relative."

"Ann asked me if. . .if I would like a suicide on my hands."

There was silence. They looked at each other. Sister Drew's face lost some of its color.

"His condition hasn't improved since I wrote to you," she said slowly. "In fact, I couldn't understand his encouraging Beth to go home. I even tried to talk them out of it last night, but he. . .he became upset and went on about having been selfish long enough." She stopped abruptly. Jumping to her feet, she said decisively, "I don't like it."

"I don't either," admitted Gail. "I just knew I had to get here as quickly as I could." She looked at Sister Drew with a hint of wonder. "It's funny, but getting to know his children and family made him somehow a person who could love and grieve, too, instead of being the murdering monster I've thought him." Her expression changed, and she added grimly, "But he still killed them all."

Jean ignored that. "Will you come over and see him with me?" she asked bluntly.

Gail hesitated. "I guess that's what I have to do. But I still don't know if I can assure him that I don't blame him, or if I can forgive. . . ."

Her voice had hardened. That had been her biggest worry about going to see the man. Would it make his depression worse if she couldn't. . .couldn't. . . .

She looked up pleadingly at Sister Drew, who said thoughtfully, "When he first became obsessed with the idea of seeing you, I did not really think that forgiveness was what he wanted from you. Since then, I've often thought there was some other reason."

Gail stared at her in surprise. "But what other reason could there be? He was drunk and they—"

"He was *not* drunk!"

"Oh, I know the police tried to tell me something like that, but I heard—"

"I don't care what you heard! Arthur was not drunk! Merciful heavens, don't tell me all this time you've thought that?"

Gail had never seen Sister Drew so angry. She gaped at her.

"That was only one senseless observation made by some stupid idiot glory seeking in front of television cameras— trying to make out he was first on the scene. It was emphatically denied by the police at the time. I repeat, Arthur had not been drinking. He had been driving trucks for years, and although he has a heap of faults, drinking has never been one of them!"

Gail was dazed. "But all this time I was sure—"

"All this time you've been sure of nothing. And we've all been a pack of senseless idiots trying to protect you while you've been so shocked by the whole wretched business!"

Sister Drew stood up and strode over to the window. Her rigid back gradually relaxed as she let the anger drain out of her. At last, she turned to Gail, who stared back blindly.

Gail was trying to remember. She had never before tried to deliberately remember those few minutes before the smash. She had always shied away from trying to remember anything after getting into the car and waving goodbye to Ann. There had been something, though. If only she could remember!

"It will all come out at the long delayed inquest eventually," Sister Drew said firmly. "Gail, the brakes on the truck failed. Apparently they had been checked before taking on that load, but they failed a couple of minutes before your father's car came around that curve." She went to add something else and thought better of it. "It's well past the time when you should have gone to the police and asked them for a few facts yourself. Now, I don't think we should waste any more time before going over to see him."

Gail stood up. She was still very pale. Sister Drew hesitated for a moment and then compressed her lips together and moved to the door.

When they reached Arthur's room, they paused.

"I think it might be best if I saw him by myself, Sister."

"No way," Sister Drew said in her best battle-ax voice and pushed open the door.

"Good afternoon, Arthur," she said loudly as she strode into the room, "I've brought you a visitor."

"Oh, no, not another of your 'cheer up poor Arthur' games, Sister Drew," a tired voice said rudely.

Gail had nursed paraplegic patients so she was quite prepared for all the paraphernalia in the room needed by someone whose body couldn't move from the waist down. What she wasn't prepared for was the thin, drawn face with Robbie's mop of curly blond hair and Jacky's hazel eyes.

He had lifted his head to see who was entering the room, and then very slowly he let it drop back onto the pillows without taking his eyes off them. Those strangely familiar eyes clung to Gail's face. A faint spark of interest lit them for a moment before he turned his head away.

"For a moment I thought I knew you," he muttered.

Sister Drew opened her mouth to say something and then resolutely closed it again.

After a few moments, when neither woman had spoken—Gail because she could not—Arthur looked at her again. A slow flush crept into his yellow cheeks. "I do know you. It's Abigail Brandon, isn't it?"

She nodded wordlessly.

"So you've condescended to visit the poor scum after all, have you? Well you can get out! *I* don't want to see you! It's too late," he suddenly snarled at her.

Gail's heart plunged.

Sister Drew put her hands on her hips and glowered at him. Inwardly, she began to feel excited. Arthur was more animated than he had been for weeks.

"She's not going anywhere. She's just flown about a thousand kilometers to see you, and the least you can do is say hello for a couple of minutes." She reached out and pulled Gail closer to the bed, pushed a chair next to her, and plonked her down in it.

She's getting quite expert at sitting me down, Gail thought a little hysterically.

"You have a lot to talk about. She's got some crazy ideas about the crash and I want you to tell her what happened. You made such a fuss for so long about seeing her I suggest you stop acting like a two-year-old boy and sort some things out." She marched to the door, turned, and unexpectedly smiled lovingly at them both before disappearing.

"Phew! I didn't know she could blow up like that," Gail said.

Arthur had lifted his head and watched the proceedings with grim astonishment. He looked at Gail searchingly.

"You. . .you should have known her when I was one of her students," Gail said huskily, hardly realizing what she was saying. "You look amazingly like Robbie," she blurted out irrelevantly.

He looked startled. "Robbie? When did you see him?"

"I've just spent several weeks looking after him—and Jacky."

An intense yearning flickered into his eyes. He opened his mouth to say something, and then tightly clamped it shut. A wary look came over his face and there was an uneasy silence while they studied each other.

"How did you know who I am?" ventured Gail at last,

then remembered, and bit her lip. "I. . .I suppose you've seen the same photograph your wife has. The one in the newspaper after. . .after the accident."

"Photo? Oh, no. Everyone has tried to spare the poor paralyzed patient. No one let a newspaper near me for a long time after the accident." His voice was very bitter.

Gail muttered, "Me, too." He narrowed his eyes at that, and she rushed on to ask, "Then how did you recognize me?"

He looked at her blankly, and then said with amazement, "You really don't remember, do you?"

"Remember? I know very little apparently!" It was her turn to sound bitter. "I wouldn't let anyone tell me anything, and so, according to Sister Drew, I've got some crazy ideas."

Arthur studied her closely for a few moments, and then closed his eyes and moved his head restlessly.

"Oh well, nothing matters now," Gail thought she heard him mutter to himself.

Alarm touched her but, before she could respond, he spoke again in a very quiet, controlled voice.

"What do you want me to tell you?"

Gail stared at him silently. Nothing. She wanted him to tell her nothing. Perspiration began beading up on her forehead. She just wanted to be able to go and forget him and the smash and everything. But at the same time. . .there had been something in his voice a moment ago. She knew she had to try to get him talking, find out if he was planning anything.

Her tongue moistened her suddenly dry lips before she said, "I want to know why you were so obsessed about seeing me."

A harsh laugh broke from him. The eyes turned to her were filled with contempt for her, for himself, for the whole world. Gail caught her breath.

"Obsessed! I suppose I was. And that's funny, now. Really funny."

But not even the hint of a smile reached his hazel eyes. They were cold as ice. He studied her carefully. She shivered.

"You look as though you've recovered enough now. There doesn't seem any need to tell you anymore." With little interest, he watched the puzzled expression that entered her face with little interest. The same harsh excuse for a laugh twisted his lips and then he turned his head and stared at the ceiling again.

"Tell me. Tell me what?" asked Gail.

He was so still for so long that she opened her mouth to insist on an answer but, at the same time, he suddenly stirred and spoke as though each word was forced out.

"I was so terribly sorry for you. Your whole family gone. Wiped out. But I needed to tell you. . . ." He paused.

When he continued, his voice had become harsher as though he, too, hated having to remember.

"It wasn't my fault. The brakes on the truck had failed just before that last bend. Sure, the truck was going too fast. But I know that stretch of road. There's a safety ramp just a few yards farther on. I had to use it once before to stop a runaway. I'd have made it this time, too, only for that car—" He broke off again and suddenly pushed himself onto one elbow and glared at Gail. "Do you have any idea why your car suddenly swerved right into me?"

For a moment, the question did not register. Gail stared at him. Her silence seemed to infuriate him.

"Well, do you?" he snapped at her.

She numbly shook her head. That acted like a time fuse. Suddenly, his words were hitting out at her, savage fury in every part of him.

"I've been lying here all these months doing nothing but think and think. Was there anything else I could have done? It all happened so fast. The brakes failed. That car coming over the double lines. A car full of people wiped out. All except one! And that such a poor specimen of a person that she wouldn't even let me see her, let alone breathe a word of thanks that I didn't let her burn to death—"

Gail was on her feet. He chopped off the last word, reprimanding himself for letting slip the one thing he had stubbornly refused to admit even to the police. With horror, he watched the effect his words had on the white-faced woman. Her body was starting to shake. She leaned against his bed as though she would fall without support.

"What. . .what are you saying? Burn to death? But that was only a dream. . .not real. . .no, no, no!"

Gail's voice had started off as though she had been running, and then, as the realization of what he had said struck her like a blow, she was screaming at him.

Arthur's horror-stricken face receded as a black mist came down.

Her body slipped to the floor.

eleven

Arthur's trembling fingers could not find his buzzer. It was
Sister Drew who burst into the room first.

"What have you done to her, Arthur? How could you!"
she roared at him while her hands were loosening Gail's
clothing, feeling for a pulse, helping the other nurses to
bring her out of the faint.

Arthur's voice was shaky and indignant. "I haven't done
a thing! She didn't seem to know anything about the fire.
Just keeled right over after scaring the living daylights out
of me."

Gail stirred, and felt a glass being held to her lips. Sister
Drew's voice commanded her to swallow. She automatically obeyed and, after a while, opened dazed eyes and
looked up at the concerned faces."

"Lie still for a bit, dear. You fainted."

Terror flooded Gail's eyes as she remembered. She
struggled to sit up.

"No, no. Where's Arthur? He's got to tell me. Did they
all die when. . .or. . .or. . .?"

Sister Drew yielded and helped her back into the chair
beside the bed. With a curt nod she dismissed the nurses,
who reluctantly went out, obviously longing to stay and
watch the drama about to take place.

Gail was staring at Arthur. He saw the torment in her
face. For the first time he caught a glimpse of the agony

this woman had been through and his own expression changed.

"You poor kid," he said very softly, "you poor, poor kid."

"Tell me," she pleaded. "I've had nightmares. I could never remember what was in them that frightened me so much. But now. . .," she brushed a hand across her eyes, "now I'm beginning to remember. The car was on fire, wasn't it? Someone was screaming. I. . .I tried to go back but he wouldn't let me. It was you, wasn't it? You. . .you. Oh, tell me! Please!"

Arthur forgot that Sister Drew was still there staring at them with blank amazement. He reached out and gripped Gail's hand tightly.

"It's all right, it's all right. There was nothing you could have done. They were all dead. Killed instantly I guess, I knew that before I heard you moan. In fact, I thought at first you were all. . . . Somehow, you were under the back seat. You were. . .were. . . ."

His hand convulsed on hers. The stench of blood and petrol was in his nostrils again. Then the smoke had drifted by. He had increased his frantic efforts to free her trapped legs. He closed his eyes and could see again the horror he could never tell this woman about. The crushed body he had managed to drag off her. It had probably protected her—the reason why she had not been killed. He could never tell her any of that.

"You dragged me from the car. But. . .but. . .the screaming?" Gail's lips could hardly move, but she never took her eyes off Art.

He looked at her. "You were screaming. I think I might

have been, too. But no one left in the car was screaming. I swear it."

Gail closed her eyes and sagged in the chair. Vaguely, she knew Sister Drew took over after that. She was insisting that Art could tell her anything else she wanted to know another time.

"There is a little more, I guess. But it can wait now," Gail heard Art agree.

Gail insisted she could walk. She stood up and swayed slightly. She resisted the grip on her arm for a moment and looked down at the man on the bed.

"You will be here tomorrow?" she whispered.

Shock made him freeze. The knowledge in her eyes left him speechless. Their eyes clung. At last he nodded. She relaxed, and let herself be led away.

Sister Drew took her straight to her own bedroom at the Nurses' Home. Not a word had been spoken until the door was closed.

"I want you to lie down on my bed and have a rest," Gail was told firmly.

She was only too thankful to submit to Sister Drew's gentle fussing. After careful questioning, she was stood over until she had eaten a small nourishing meal, which eventually helped to stop her trembling.

At last Sister Drew left her in peace while she raced down to her office to use the phone. Miss Fisher listened to her carefully and finally agreed to Jean's request for Gail to use an empty room in the Home.

"And you could tell her I would like to see her tomorrow sometime if she's up to it. A junior sister from Men's Medical has just handed me her resignation, and she might like to apply for the position. Oh, and there was a phone call concerning Sister Brandon. Just a moment." A brief pause, and Sister Drew heard the rustle of papers. "I intended to contact you later. It was a Reverend Diamond. Said he had only just returned from overseas and had been told about the accident. Was most anxious to speak to her."

Sister Drew carefully wrote down the phone number he had left for Gail to contact him.

The next call she made was long distance. Sister Drew spoke briefly to Marian Stevens and then listened intently. As she did so, her face began to light up, and when she eventually replaced the receiver, she sat for a few moments in deep thought.

Gail was sitting on the side of the bed when Sister Drew at last returned to the room. She looked up at her blankly.

"I've been remembering what happened in the car just before. . .just before. . . ." she swallowed painfully.

Sister Drew moved to sit beside her and put a comforting arm around her. She waited patiently.

Gail fought for control, closing her eyes tightly. "We'd been talking about the wedding. Bill was bored, and watching Dad's driving. Mum always carried some sweets or biscuits. I was trying to get her bag when Bill suddenly yelled." Gail's eyes flew open. "Perhaps that startled Dad," she whispered. "Bill was leaning over the seat right next to him."

Sister Drew's arm tightened slightly, but she remained silent, allowing the memories to surface at last.

"I'd undone my seat belt and was right down on the floor. I don't know how it happened." There was another pause and then she concluded sadly, "There was something Wayne was going to tell me, too. When we got home. Guess I'll never know what it was now."

Sister Drew still waited patiently, and eventually Gail stirred and turned with sudden resolution to face her.

"Sister Drew, there's something I want to ask you. There was an old man on the plane this afternoon. He. . .he told me God loves me and longs for me to turn to Him. He said to reach out to Him and. . .and. . . . I need Him so much, but I don't know how. . .or. . . . I've been learning so much about God these past few weeks." Her eyes filled with a great yearning. "Jim. . . ."

The way she choked on his name brought a gleam to Sister Drew's eyes that she hastily veiled as Gail stumbled on.

"Jim said once that he had handed over complete control of his life to Jesus Christ. Do you know if that is what the old man may have meant? Is that why you and Jim and his mother are so different from so many other religious people I've met? Like Aunt Harriet?"

There had been many times when Sister Drew had visited Gail in the hospital and had prayed and longed to talk to her about Christ as she did during the next half-hour or so. There were many questions from Gail and many answers found in the slightly battered Bible that Sister Drew picked up from the bedside table.

Gail carefully watched her as she talked and explained. The words she quoted from the Bible were burned deeply into Gail's heart and mind by the light that shone in her face and the ring of conviction and certainty that rang gloriously in her voice.

That same certainty and light had been Jim's the day he

had preached. It had been Marian Stevens's when she had answered Gail's questions. And it had been in the old man—a total stranger.

Finally, Sister Drew rose to her feet and looked lovingly and longingly down at Gail.

"There's so much more I could share with you, Gail, so much more God has to teach us both in the future. We don't know why God allows tragedy to strike at us, but we do know He loves us. Above all, remember that the proof we have of His love for all time is the death of Christ on the cross. God allowed that suffering, too. But He was also there—in the suffering. If you take that first step and ask Christ to come into your life, then He will become your teacher. I'm afraid it all boils down to faith. If you really believe that He is God's Son, and wants you to let Him have control of your life, and wants you to share an intimate relationship with Him, then you will do what He wants you to—you will obey Him. Only then will it be possible for Him to pour out His blessings and promises upon you the way He wants to. He will give you a whole new life and purpose for living. And you'll never be alone again."

She paused. Gail's face was very pale and drawn. She was looking down at her hands as they fiddled with a well-crumpled handkerchief.

"Now, my dear," Jean said gently. "I think you've had enough for one day. I've organized a room here in the Home for you and you can go and settle down there and think about it all in peace and privacy."

By the time Gail fell into bed that evening, she was too weary to try to sort it all out. As she snuggled into the soft pillow, her last waking thought was of the love on the old man's face as he told her that God loved her.

With her eyes closed, a deep, heartfelt prayer rose to her lips in the simple whisper of a child.

"Thank You, for loving me so much."

And then she slept deeply and without dreams until the early morning sun crept through her window.

Gail stirred and stretched luxuriously. It had been quite early when she had gone to bed, and she glanced at her watch to see that it was not yet time for the first shift of nurses to be up and scurrying into their uniforms.

She felt relaxed and rested as she had not felt for a very long time. A sense of well-being enveloped her as she turned over and looked around at the familiar bareness of the room. It was so typical of the other rooms she had occupied for years.

As she lay there, she remembered the way she had felt the day she had thought she had said goodbye to rooms like this. A slight smile stirred her lips as she thought of Ann's reaction to her sentimental tears.

That memory led to others. She got out of bed and went across to the window. It was a glorious new morning, the early rays of the sun just beginning to glisten on the trees in a nearby park. She stood there for a few moments, her heart full. Then she lifted her gaze a little and saw the small building tucked away among some trees.

Swiftly, she reached for her clothes and hurriedly dressed before making her way to that small building. It was the hospital chapel. She hesitated in the doorway. It was never locked and, as she sat down in a pew near the door, she felt ashamed that in all her years at the Nurses' Home she had never before ventured inside.

She looked around her. Soft lighting revealed the tasteful furnishings. There was a small platform with an altar. Gail thought briefly of the many people who, over the years, had come in here seeking God while their loved ones lived or died in the wards nearby.

She wondered if Beth and Jim had been here.

With a sigh, Gail leaned her head against the cool cement wall. She thought of Beth's angry, bitter words and then, with a feeling of relief and release, she remembered the love and acceptance in Marian Stevens's eyes and arms. She pushed thoughts of Jim away and dwelt on Sister Drew's words of the night before.

She closed her eyes, but the slow tears forced their way past her eyelids and trickled down her cheeks. Her whole body yearned for that God Who loved her.

The minutes passed in that quiet place. Not even the hum of the awakening city intruded. Gradually, Gail began to feel that she was not alone. The sensation became so strong her figure tensed, her eyes flew open, and she glanced around. The chapel was empty.

"You'll never be alone again."

Sister Drew's words. Wonderful words.

When eventually Gail moved again and raised the head that had been bowed for countless moments, she did not realize that in her face shone the same brilliance that had lit up Sister Drew the night before. She only knew a great sense of peace and relief.

Reluctantly, she at last rose to her feet and, as she turned towards the door, noticed for the first time the painting hanging on the back wall. She peered at it for a moment, and then abruptly moved closer.

She was right. It was the same portrait of Christ that hung in Jim's bedroom. The beads of sweat glistened on the strong forehead above the eyes that she had often thought about when Christ had been mentioned.

Whether it was the soft lighting or her own imagination she was not sure, but it seemed that this painting reflected even more of His strength and tenderness as He looked at her.

When Gail at last emerged from the chapel, the sun had strengthened and hurrying nurses were making their way across to relieve the tired night staff. She lingered for a while, under the trees, looking about her. Perhaps this was where God wanted her to be. She had an appointment to see Miss Fisher later on. For a moment, a great longing for those sun-drenched black soil plains swept through her.

And for Jim.

She lifted her chin and straightened her shoulders. The old man's Friend had not let him down for over sixty years. Her new Friend would give her the strength to cope.

Later on in the morning, Sister Drew looked keenly at Gail as she walked into her office. The strain was gone from her eyes. She was at peace. There was a spring in her stride that told of purpose and hope. For a moment, she wondered if the change in her was merely the result of a good night's sleep and the release of tension. Then, with an endearing touch of bashfulness, Gail smiled gently at Sister Drew.

Gail stared in embarrassed surprise at the tears that began to slowly trickle down the lined face. Sister Drew brushed them away with the back of her hand, stood up, and walked around her desk to draw Gail close and kiss her gently.

"I'm just so glad, my dear," was all that she said.

They looked at each other and Gail's lips at last twitched. Sister Drew gave a smothered laugh as she reached for a tissue and wiped her eyes. They beamed at each other.

"Well! I never thought the day would come when Sister Drew would cry all over me," Gail said daringly.

It was Sister Drew's turn to look a little embarrassed as she turned back to her desk. "It's the first time someone I have been talking to about the Lord has become a Christian," she retorted.

Her experience was still too new and wonderful for Gail to talk about, so she said swiftly, "Do you think I'd be allowed to see Art now?"

"Most certainly." Sister Drew's voice regained its usual crispness. "I've already rung the Nursing Unit Manager and gained permission for you to go and see him at any time. And have you rung that Reverend Diamond yet?"

"No," Gail said reluctanctly. "He was the minister at the church back home where Mum sometimes went." She paused, and then burst out with, "I want to talk to Art first. I realize now there's so much I don't know about the accident. Oh, Sister Drew, I'm so ashamed about my utter selfishness. If I'd gone to see him before, when you begged me to, so much anguish could have been avoided. Beth would not have been so bitter and. . .and Jim. . . ." She stopped short and stared miserably at Sister Drew. "Art was right. I'm a poor specimen of a person. I. . . ."

"You *were*, Gail. You were. Not now. Remember that now you're a new person. That's all in the past. Certainly the effects of the past can still be there, but you, yourself, have a new beginning."

Gail stared at her. A new beginning. A new Friend. A new Life. It was true. Sister Drew thrilled at the light that began to warm the dark eyes until they glowed with a deep fire.

"Thank you," Gail said softly. She made her way to the door and then turned and smiled at Sister Drew. "Thank you," she said fervently, and then was gone.

The door to Arthur's room was propped open when Gail arrived. A beaming nurse coming out of the room eyed her curiously, but cheerfully told her to go straight in as her patient had been fretting to see her all morning.

"I thought you'd be here ages ago," Art scowled at her as she approached his bed.

They eyed each other silently. Gail was relieved to see how friendly his eyes were behind the scowl. His face was less drawn and pale than the day before. Unexpectedly, he grinned at her.

"Sit down, please. And don't you dare faint on me again or darling Sister Jean Drew will eat me for dinner."

Gail didn't move. She moistened her lips and began to say, "I want to say how sorry I am for—"

He scowled at her again as he rudely interrupted. "Please, keep quiet and sit down."

Gail sat. She gripped her fingers together and tried again. "I can't shut up. I've behaved despicably and caused you a lot more pain than you already had and—"

Arthur raised a thin hand and shook it at her. "If you don't stop at once, I'll ring the bell and get you kicked out," he said ferociously.

She stared at him helplessly.

His face softened again. "There was plenty of excuse for you, you poor kid."

Gail looked down at her hands.

He straightened the sheet across his chest and cleared his throat. "Er. . .look, there's a lot to talk about and I don't want those nurses to know. Would you mind closing the door so they can't hear us?"

When Gail had sat down again, he was frowning as he examined his fingernails. She could not think of a single thing to say, and sat studying him until he shot a glance at her and said abruptly, "What did you mean yesterday when you asked me if I would still be here today?"

Gail tensed, searching very carefully for the right words. "Two days, ago I received a couple of letters that told me that certain people looking after you were afraid that you were becoming too depressed and might. . .might. . . ."

He was still looking at his hands while she paused, hesitant to say more, and then he raised his head and looked at her. "And then I sent Beth home and after I spoke to you the way I did you were convinced they were right?"

She nodded slowly.

He sighed. "Nothing seemed worthwhile anymore. I was sick of pain. . .sick of being a cripple. . . ." His voice was low and full of anguish. "I'd already made a mess of our marriage. I'll never know why Beth loves me. But she does, and she's a very fine woman. Too fine to have to put up with me. I could see what it was doing to her, having to chose between me and the kids, seeing me here day after day. I couldn't stand it any longer." He stopped abruptly.

Gail waited for him to continue, and then she asked softly, "And now?"

"Now?" He looked at her intently. "After you went last night I suddenly saw myself as the coward I really am," he said with self-loathing. "It was just the easy way out."

Gail swallowed and forced herself to say shyly, "Weren't you afraid of meeting God in such a way?"

He stared at her. "Don't tell me you believe all that religious stuff that Beth does?"

She nodded briefly.

"Well, how do you like that."

"It's all very new to me, I'm afraid, and I'm not sure if I can explain any of it yet, but—"

"And don't you try, either," Art exploded. "After we were married, Beth nagged me more than anything else about God and going to church. I can't believe in her God of love and that's final!"

Gail was so startled she blurted out before she stopped to think, "Well! If it wasn't for the way I've been gradually learning about God, I'd never have come to see you yesterday, and you could have been dead—oh!"

Gail gasped and put her hand up to her mouth and stared at him with appalled eyes.

There was a tense silence.

"I guess you could be right at that," Art at last said very softly in a shaking voice.

"Oh, I'm so sorry for saying that the way I did, I—"

"Please, stop saying you're sorry." He cleared his throat. Then, in a strained voice, he said, "Open that top drawer of the locker and find a hard-covered book shoved to the back."

Gail stared at him blankly until he glared at her and said fiercely, "Do it! Please!"

When she turned back to the bed with the book in her hand, she gazed down at him in stunned amazement. Carefully, between several pages of a large book, he had stored quite a number of tablets of different shapes and sizes.

"I'd worked it out—some are antibiotics that I didn't want to stop the infections. But I'd worked it out that, with the pain tablets and sleeping pills for last night, there should have been just enough. Instead, I swallowed the ones given to me last night and had the best sleep since I don't know when," he added shamedly. Then, in a mild panic, "Please, throw those things down the sink. Quickly, before a nurse comes in."

Gail shook the book over the sink until she was sure all the tablets were gone, then turned on the tap and washed them away.

Art breathed a sigh of relief.

"I just don't understand how you could have fooled the nurses so many times!" Gail said incredulously.

He grinned weakly. "It wasn't easy. And some nurses I couldn't do it with—stood over me with beady eyes. And sometimes the pain was just so bad. . . . I made up for that by asking for them when I didn't really need them. So, it took a bit longer than I thought." His face sobered and, for a moment, he looked haunted as he added, "I didn't know how long a night could be."

Gail returned the book to the locker and sat down again.

"Let's not mention it again," Art said. "I've been in a panic to know how to get rid of them, but then I figured you might understand. . . . That's all over now. Finished." He swallowed and said slowly, "I guess you really came to see me to hear about the accident."

"I've been able to remember, since seeing you, the last few minutes before the smash," Gail managed to say at last. She still felt very shaken, and knew she would in the future always be one of those beady-eyed nurses!

Art looked at her speculatively. "Do you know, in some peculiar way, it was a relief to talk about it yesterday. Even though you fainted, I felt as though a great weight had gone after you left."

"Well, Sister Drew seems to think that now that I know what. . .," Gail gulped, "what you told me about the fire, I'll probably not have any more nightmares. It's still very difficult to talk about it all, but there's something I've thought about since that doesn't make sense."

Gail paused. Neither took any notice of the heavy footsteps in the corridor. Gail had her back to the door, and Arthur had removed his eyes from her face as she spoke and closed them.

Neither heard the door pushed slowly open as Gail continued, "How could you have pulled me from the wreck when you were so badly injured yourself?"

There was silence for a moment, and then a deep voice spoke from the doorway.

"That's something I'd very much like to know, too."

Art's face lit up. "Jim!" he yelled.

twelve

Gail froze while Jim took a few more steps into the room and came to the other side of Art's bed and into her line of vision.

"How are you, Art?" His voice was polite, if a little mechanical.

Unfortunately, Jim wasn't even looking at the man on the bed. Blue eyes were locked with dazed brown ones.

Gail stared at the tall brown man in the familiar brown suit. It couldn't be. He was in Queensland. He was on the header.

She must have said so, because white teeth showed briefly for a moment, and it was Jim's voice that said gently, "I'm not, you know. Mr. Garrett is."

Hilda's father. Gail blinked rapidly, and then lowered her eyes.

"You didn't stop running so I had to come to you," the quiet voice said, and her eyes flew to meet his again.

Art had been looking from one to another in surprise. At last his eyes lit with amusement.

"Hey! I thought visitors to poor sick invalids came to see them—not each other," he said in a plaintive voice.

Gail blushed scarlet and tore her eyes away from Jim.

"We...er...didn't say goodbye properly," said Jim with a laugh in his voice. He pulled up a chair and sat down. With his chin resting on his hands as he leaned on the bed, he looked searchingly at Art. "You look a lot better than I expected after what Beth has said."

Art and Gail looked at each other. His eyes pleaded with her not to say anything.

"I guess it's the pretty visitor I have," he said quickly.

Jim looked suspiciously from one to the other. "You appeared to be having a very interesting conversation when I walked in."

Arthur looked embarrassed, and then suddenly alarmed. "How long were you in the room?"

"I heard Gail ask you a question." Jim's eyes narrowed as Art relaxed. "Apparently, she seems to think that you pulled her from the wreck."

"Well," said Art a little too quickly and a little too casually, "I was just about to ask her what on earth she was talking about when you burst in."

Gail stared at him "But yesterday you said—"

Art interrupted her swiftly. "Yesterday you fainted, remember?"

"Fainted?" Jim exclaimed with concern.

"Apparently she didn't remember anything about the accident, and I'm afraid something I said shocked her."

"Was it about the fire?" Jim asked abruptly.

Gail's eyes widened. "How did you know?" she gasped.

"That nightmare you had, remember? You were yelling out something. I've given a lot of thought to that since I found out who you were." He stopped.

"I'm so sorry about all the deception, Jim," Gail said huskily after a pause.

Art watched curiously as Jim smiled at her and relief flashed into her face. "Hmmmm. It seems there are things

I don't know," he complained.

"You'll no doubt hear all about it from Beth," Jim said rapidly. "Now, stop trying to sidetrack us. About Gail's question—what did you think Art said yesterday, Gail?"

Art started to protest again, but Jim ignored him and looked at Gail.

Something here was not quite right. Gail looked from one to another with a puzzled frown.

"Art said he pulled me out of the car just before it. . . it . . . ." she swallowed. "I only vaguely remember anything at all after the impact. But someone was pulling me and. . . ." she wiped a hand across her eyes.

There was silence. Art's thin cheeks were tinged with pink. Jim watched him closely.

"This interests me profoundly, Gail. You see, the police and doctors were rather puzzled. They didn't know how you could have received the type of injuries you had when Art kept insisting you must have been thrown out of the car."

"Thrown out! But Art, you said—" She stopped abruptly.

"What did he tell you, Gail?" Jim's voice had hardened.

She opened her mouth to answer him but Art suddenly cut in. "Please, don't make the poor kid go through all that again," he said roughly. "Okay. I acted the big hero."

There was silence. Art stared determinedly at the ceiling. He was very pale.

"You can't just leave it at that, I'm afraid, old man." Jim's voice was very gentle. "Couldn't you tell us a bit more?"

Gail held her breath and expelled it slowly as Art began to talk in a painfully disjointed voice.

It appeared that the car had been tossed off the huge bull-bars of the truck and then it had turned into the embankment beside the road. The truck had only jack-knifed and Art had merely been bruised and badly shaken. He had run over to the mess of glass and metal that had once been a car, not really thinking that anyone could have survived. The smell of petrol was strong and he had just noticed a wisp of smoke when he heard someone moan. He had managed to drag her a only few feet when the car burst into flames. Gail had come to a little and started to fight him. Suddenly, the petrol tank had exploded and something hit him in the back.

Art only told them the bare facts that morning. Later, when Gail talked to the police and ambulance crew, she found out that Art had fallen across her own body and shielded her from the fire. The grass near them had caught fire. The first rescuer on the scene had arrived just in time to beat out the flames as Art's clothes caught fire and prevented Art from being more severely burned than he had been. Even then, the burns had been bad enough to cause added problems in the treatment of his back.

When Art finished talking, he flung one arm up across his eyes and the two listeners saw his chest heave and heard one hard, dry sob burst from him.

There were tears running down Gail's own cheeks. Instinctively, she stood up and sat on the bed and put her arms around Art.

"Oh, Art," she murmured. "Thank you, so much. And I'm so sorry that you were so badly hurt saving my life."

Art tolerated her comforting arms for a few moments and then pushed her away. "I thought I told you to shut up about that 'sorry' business," he muttered.

Jim was the first to recover and adroitly changed the subject by starting to tell Arthur about the harvest. Some of his old truckie mates had been driving semitrailers carrying grain, Gail discovered as she listened quietly. Jim rambled on for a while until both Gail and Arthur had recovered and composed themselves.

Then, Jim looked at Gail and announced casually, "By the way, Gail, you'll be interested to know that while we were in Brisbane yesterday, Mum killed a large brown snake."

Gail exclaimed in horror.

"Where abouts, Jim?" asked Arthur with interest.

"Near the laundry door." Jim grinned at Gail's expression. "Don't look so frightened. Be thankful it wasn't curled up in a pile of dirty clothes when you were doing the washing. We think it must have been after some of the milk left out for Bonnie."

"I bet Mum broke her clothesline prop again," Art said with a grin. Jim nodded, and both men chuckled.

"She always grabs the longest weapon she can find," Art explained to Gail. "She reckons she's busted every prop she's ever had over the years killing snakes."

Gail thought of the clothesline prop she had often used. It had been at least eight feet long. "I don't think I could even get that close to a snake to kill it," shuddered Gail.

Jim's expression sobered. "If you knew it was around where the children played, and that next time it could bite one of them, you would."

They were all silent for a moment. Jim was looking intently at Gail. "Gail hates snakes," he said softly to

Arthur without taking his eyes off her.

Gail felt warmth creeping into her cheeks again. She lifted her chin and looked Jim straight in the eye. It wasn't she that had anything to be ashamed of that night she had nearly stepped on the snake.

Arthur glanced from Gail to Jim—they were absorbed in each other. His lips twitched and he began to laugh softly.

They both turned and stared at him as he muttered, "Well, well." He tried to turn the laugh into a cough behind one hand. "Er, yes. Interesting topic. . .er. . .snakes," he said very rapidly. His eyes were dancing. "Jim, do you remember the black one your dog, Toby, flushed out?"

He launched quickly into a snake yarn, giving Gail a chance to recover again.

After that, Arthur wanted to know all about Jacky and Robbie. His face softened while they told him about the chicken pox episode and their antics with the collie pup. Whatever the children's feelings about their father, it was obvious that he was hungry for news of them.

There was a shadow on Arthur's face as Gail assured him that Jacky had no scars on her face from the scabs. She wondered if the children's illness had not been the last straw for him in his already depressed state.

The physiotherapist arrived shortly afterwards to "do her torturing," as Arthur put it. Jim and Gail rose at once.

Gail reached out and gently touched one of Art's thin white hands. "I'll be back when I can to tell you all about my time up there," she promised with a sympathetic smile.

"I'll see you again before I go home tonight, mate," Jim said as he reached out and shook Art's hand.

"Yeah, you do that." A twinkle sprang into life in the eyes so much like his son's. "And then you can tell me when the wedding's going to be," he drawled softly.

Gail heard and nearly tripped on her way to the door. She didn't see Jim's look of utter amazement. Then, a dark tide of red swept over his face as he glared at his brother-in-law. Jim muttered something Gail didn't hear, but Art was chuckling out loud as he followed Gail outside the room.

Gail went striding off down the corridor and Jim didn't catch up with her until she stopped and jabbed the button for the lift. When she turned to face him, her chin was tilted, her eyes turbulent.

Before he could speak, she said quickly, "I'm afraid I've an appointment with the Director of Nursing very shortly. There's a job available for me. I don't think I'll have much time to see you before you go home. With uniforms and things to organize," she ended a little lamely.

"But Gail," he began urgently, "I came to see you. To take you back. Mum wants—"

The lift doors opened and several people crowded past them. He opened his mouth again, but she broke in, knowing her self-control wouldn't be able to take much more.

"I'm not going back, Jim. I'm sorry, but that was only a job to tide me over." She stepped into the lift.

He followed her and glared at a couple of unfortunate nurses who joined them. "Gail, we've got to talk," he began desperately as the lift doors closed. His hand smoothing over his face in the old characteristic way was the last straw.

"Not today, Jim," Gail's voice trembled. The lift stopped. "Nursing Administration is on this floor. Good...goodbye. I hope you and Hilda. . .your wedding plans. . .be happy. . . ."

She couldn't look at him as she brushed past and raced off down the corridor, around a corner and out of sight. Tears were blurring her vision. She had once worked on this floor, and she went through a swinging door and then found herself in a linen room. It took her a couple of minutes to gain control, but she knew there was no way she could keep her interview with Miss Fisher. A nurse burst into the room; Gail straightened, murmured an apology, and retreated.

She headed for the stairs and on the next floor found a phone. After dialing Miss Fisher's office and asking for the appointment to be changed to the next day, she headed for the lifts again, trying not to think of Jim. She thrust her hand into the pocket in her skirt and felt the piece of paper on which Sister Drew Jean Drew had written Reverend Diamond's phone number. She had met him several times over the years, and suddenly desperately needed to talk to someone who had known her family.

On the ground floor she made for the public phones.

When she at last hung up, the tears were pouring down her face again—but this time from utter wonder and joy. Outside, the sun streamed down as she lifted her radiant face and breathed deeply. She had to tell someone. Sister Drew would understand. But first. . . .

It was late in the afternoon when Sister Drew, standing at her office window, breathed a sigh of relief as she watched Gail stride across the car park towards the Nurses' Home just like she had all those weeks ago.

She had been very concerned since Jim had erupted into her office, hours before, after their visit to Art, demanding that she help him track Gail down. For a moment, she watched the steady approach of the slender figure. As she got closer, Gail looked up briefly and Sister Drew smiled thankfully at her serene expression.

Gail paused for a moment outside the open office door and listened to hear if anyone was with Sister Drew. Then, she knocked and went in.

"Sister Drew, I've got something rather wonderful to tell. . . ."

A tall figure outlined near the window swung around.

Gail stopped, and then advanced slowly. "Why, Jim, I thought you'd be gone."

"Oh, did you? And I suppose that's why you've now turned up!" The words were cold and furious.

As he moved swiftly across the room, Gail looked into his face and took a step back at the fury and frustration glaring at her from the white, grim-faced, disheveled, desperate man. He reached out and grabbed her above the elbows, hauling her close.

"Where on earth have you been, Gail! We've turned the place upside down looking for you! How dare you run away like that when I've come so far to see you!"

"Me? But. . .but. . .Jim!"

The last word was muffled as hungry, urgent lips stopped his name on her mouth. It was a relieved, angry kiss. For a moment, she was too stunned to move. Then, her lips softened and began to respond as they always would to this beloved man.

Jim wrenched his head away. Gail stilled, waiting for she knew not what. He groaned, let his painful grip on her arms go and, for one dreadful moment, she thought he was already regretting the kiss. Then, his arms were around her, pressing her close to his body, his hand in her hair, holding her head against his as their lips joined again. This time there was no mistaking the tenderness, the love, that poured from one heart to the other.

At last, they searched each other's eyes, still clinging as though the other would disappear.

"I don't understand," Gail's voice was breathless with wonder and dawning excitement. "I thought you. . .you and. . . ."

The anger had gone from his vivid blue eyes. There was no mistaking the light that blazed from them as he surveyed the rosy blush flooding Gail's bewildered face.

"I've wanted to do that ever since the night I made you cry," he murmured, then touched her lips briefly again with his as though he couldn't resist them.

Suddenly, with violence, she pushed him away from her. "Then why?" Anger and indignation started to rise in Gail. "Why did you kiss me and then be so dreadfully sorry! Why the *'please forgive me, it won't happen again'* drama," she spat at him.

One large hand wiped over his face.

"And don't *do* that!" she yelled at him.

He stared at her, the spot of color high on his cheekbones fading. "Do what?" he asked in a strained voice.

She turned her back and hunched her shoulders. "It doesn't matter," she muttered.

Gentle, hesitant hands touched her shoulders and he moved so he could see her face again. "Don't. . .don't kiss you again?"

She glared at him defiantly. "Yes! What about your wedding plans with Hilda? I do take it that was why you were so sorry?"

"Hilda?" Sheer amazement filled his face. "What on earth has she got to do with anything?" A thunderstruck expression swiftly chased the amazement away. "You mentioned her just before you ran off, didn't you? You don't think. . .? You do! Why?" His hands tightened on her.

"Because she told me!"

"Gail, we've got to talk," he said urgently.

"You've already said that!" she snapped at him, hardly daring to believe what she was thinking. "So, talk!"

He stared at her desperately. Then, he straightened. She held her breath when his hands let her go. A multitude of expressions flew across his face. Then, blue eyes were piercing her to the bone.

"Right! First, I couldn't believe my eyes when I first saw you. You were so angry and the most beautiful woman I'd ever seen. I knew from the beginning you were dangerous to my peace of mind. There was so much sadness in you, so much mystery about you. Above all, you didn't have a personal relationship with Christ. I guess I've almost developed a. . .a phobia about loving any woman who couldn't share my commitment to Him. I've seen what's happened to too many marriages where that one vital sharing is impossible. Even Beth. . . . And then, when I was beginning to wonder about that, I found out about Wayne. You can hardly bear to talk about him still."

Gail's mouth had dropped open. Her hand went out to him as remembered anguish filled his eyes. He grabbed her hand and she winced as his hand tightened.

"Please, Gail, won't you come back with me," he pleaded hoarsely. "It'll give you more time to—"

"Jim," she interrupted the staccato words, still scarcely daring yet to believe what his eyes were telling her, "Oh, Jim, I do share your love for Christ."

"I know. Aunt Jean told me when I was so upset when you disappeared. But I meant more time to get over losing Wayne, more time so that perhaps you might learn to love again. To love me. . . ."

She gasped. "Oh, Jim," she said wildly, "First Reverend Diamond tells me all my family, Wayne, too, had yielded completely to Christ's claims on their lives. There's absolutely no doubt I'll see them all again one day with Him. After lunch, I spent ages walking, sitting in the chapel, talking with God. And now. . .are you saying you . . .you love me? You want to be with me for all my tomorrows?"

"Of course I'm saying I love you. Of course I want to share with you all the tomorrows God gives us. The only wedding I'll ever be planning with anyone will be with you—no one else," he said furiously. "Surely, you must have known. Everyone else seems to. Even Arthur, after two minutes! I love you and. . . ."

Sister Drew softly approached her office, hoping against hope that leaving Jim alone before Gail had arrived would have given those two dear people a chance to sort some things out. She poked her head around the partly opened door.

Well, well, she thought as she very quietly closed the door firmly on the two young people kissing so lovingly. As she walked away, her eyes were misting, her heart singing with joy, her lips gently moving with a loving prayer.

"Oh, thank You, Lord. Bless them! Bless them!"

add a little *MYSTERY* to your romance!

TWO GREAT INSPIRATIONAL ROMANCES
WITH JUST A TOUCH OF MYSTERY
BY MARLENE J. CHASE

_____*The Other Side of Silence*—Anna Durham finds a purpose for living in the eyes of a needy child and a reason to love in the eyes of a lonely physician...but first the silence of secrets must be broken. HP6 BHSB-07 $2.95.

_____*This Trembling Cup*—A respite on a plush Wisconsin resort may just be the thing for Angie Carlson's burn-out—or just the beginning of a devious plot unraveling and the promise of love. HP5 BHSB-05 $2.95.

Inspirational Romance at its Best from one of America's Favorite Authors!

FOUR HISTORICAL ROMANCES
BY COLLEEN L. REECE

___ *A Torch for Trinity*—When Trinity Mason sacrifices her teaching ambitions for a one-room school, her life—and Will Thatcher's—will never be the same. HP1 BHSB-01 $2.95

___*Candleshine*-A sequel to *A Torch for Trinity*—With the onslaught of World War II, Candleshine Thatcher dedicates her life to nursing, and then her heart to a brave Marine lieutenant. HP7 BHSB-06 $2.95

___*Wildflower Harvest*—Ivy Ann and Laurel were often mistaken for each other...was it too late to tell one man the truth? HP2 BHSB-02 $2.95

___ *Desert Rose*-A sequel to *Wildflower Harvest*—When Rose Birchfield falls in love with one of Michael's letters, and then with a cowboy named Mike, no one is more confused than Rose herself. HP8 BHSB-08 $2.95